THIS SIDE OF MIDNIGHT

A JOHN BEKKER MYSTERY

THIS SIDE OF MIDNIGHT

AL LAMANDA

FIVE STAR

A part of Gale, Cengage Learning

GALE
CENGAGE Learning·

Farmington Hills, Mich • San Francisco • New York • Waterville, Maine
Meriden, Conn • Mason, Ohio • Chicago

GALE
CENGAGE Learning·

LIBRARY OF CONGRESS CATALOGING-IN-PUBLICATION DATA

Lamanda, Al.
   This side of midnight : a John Bekker mystery / by Al Lamanda. — First Edition.
   pages ; cm.
   ISBN 978-1-4328-3071-7 (hardcover) — ISBN 1-4328-3071-6 (hardcover)
   1. Bekker, John. 2. Private investigators—Fiction. I. Title.
PS3612.A5433T48 2015
813'.6—dc23   2014047851

First Edition. First Printing: June 2015
Find us on Facebook– https://www.facebook.com/FiveStarCengage
Visit our website– http://www.gale.cengage.com/fivestar/
Contact Five Star™ Publishing at FiveStar@cengage.com

Printed in the United States of America
1 2 3 4 5 6 7 19 18 17 16 15

THIS SIDE OF MIDNIGHT

ONE

There are some mornings where the Pacific Ocean is as blue as Paul Newman's eyes. This was one of those mornings.

Eighty-four degrees with a slight salt-sea breeze that filled your lungs and clung to your skin like mist. The tide was rolling in and the waves were dotted with surfers and a few sailboats off in the distance.

I wore shorts, a tee shirt and jogging shoes. I carried five-pound ankle weights. I removed the jogging shoes and wrapped a weight around each ankle. Then I removed the tee shirt and tossed it on top of the shoes.

I broke into a slow jog for about a quarter of a mile to allow my legs to adjust to running barefoot in wet sand. After a while I warmed up and my muscles loosened.

Then I turned it up a bit.

I lit a cigarette as I walked. This high up, the breeze off the ocean was cool and filled with salt sea air. I walked about a half-mile when I saw Melissa Koch power-walking toward me.

She held weights in each hand.

I knew I was approaching the one-mile mark into my run by the house high on the cliff to my left. I opened my stride a bit, tuned out the sounds of the ocean and entered a zone of silence.

★ ★ ★ ★ ★

She saw me and didn't break stride until the gap between us narrowed to twenty feet or so. Then she slowed to a stop.

I kept walking and stopped in front of her, blocking her path.

We looked at each other.

Her eyes were defiant.

"I should have had Herb just shoot you and be done with it," Melissa said.

"Why?"

"Because my idiot husband can't keep his dick in his pants," Melissa said. *"Because I've invested too much time and trouble in his career to let him piss the White House away on some stupid bitch with a schoolgirl crush on him. Stupid girl goes and gets herself knocked up and I'm supposed to suffer and give it all up because of it. I think not."*

"So you made her disappear?" I said.

"Yes."

"Where?"

"I don't know."

Around a mile and a half into my run I passed a young woman walking her dog along the shoreline. I'd seen them before. She wasn't much older than my daughter, Regan. The dog, a male, was a golden retriever just out of the puppy stage. He pranced out of the water and ran toward me. The woman called him back and he made an immediate U-turn.

"And Handler?"

"He's nothing." Melissa showed me a tiny grin. *"Although he proved very useful there at the end, didn't he?"*

"Herb kill him?"

"Herb hoisted his unconscious body, but as you figured out, I tied the knot in the noose," Melissa said. *"Now, as you have no proof of*

any of this and never will, I will ask you this once to leave my property. After that, I will call 911 and tell them I have an intruder."

She accented her point by holding both weights in her right hand, pulling a tiny cell phone from her waistband with her left.

"Sun's coming up," I said.

"So it is," Melissa said.

"The White House that important you'd kill for it?"

"Yes, and it's been done before," Melissa said. "Now get out of my way before I call the police."

About a mile up ahead I caught a glimpse of the palatial mansion belonging to Senator Oliver Koch of Maine, a very rich and powerful member of the Senate.

I turned up the heat and raced the mile to the side of the cliff where the mansion stood some one hundred feet-plus above it.

I stepped aside.

She looked me in the eye. "Speak one word of this and my attorneys will take away all that you have and all that you ever will have, including that girlfriend of yours and your pretty little daughter. Understood?"

"Yes."

The grin reappeared. "Good day, Mr. Bekker."

I took a deep breath and filled my lungs with salt-sea air.

The breeze was cool on my face.

Off on the horizon just a tiny sliver of sunlight brightened the dark sky.

The first light of a new day gave the promise of hope and potential.

I had regained my soul not yet a year ago and I wasn't prepared to lose it again. Third chances are few and far between. I closed my eyes for a brief moment. My inner voice told me what the right thing to do was.

My eyes opened.

The look in Melissa Koch's eyes told me I was already dismissed.

At the three-mile marker of Koch's mansion, I turned right and entered the water about a foot deep, and started the return run. Almost immediately the ankle weights took on water and doubled in weight.

I took a step to my right to allow her to pass.

Waves from the rising tide crashed against my legs and the run grew increasingly difficult. About a half mile into the return trip the muscles in my thighs started to ache and burn from lactic acid buildup. I fought through it and tried to keep the same pace despite fifteen pounds of weight around each ankle.

As Melissa Koch stepped around me her left foot brushed my left ankle. She stumbled forward, lost her balance and tumbled to her left. I turned to catch her, but her forward momentum carried her to the soft dirt at the edge of the cliff where she landed with a thud.
  I spun around.
  "Are you all right?" I said.
  "Yes, you buffoon, I am all right and no thanks to you."
  "Let me give you a hand." I started walking to the edge.
  "I don't need your help," Melissa Koch said.

I was a mile from completing the round-trip. My back hurt from having to lift my legs high out of the water. The ever-rising tide and waves pushed at me with each stride.
  My arms and shoulders ached.
  My legs burned.
  My lungs were on fire.

★　★　★　★　★

I stopped about six or seven feet from her.

Slowly, Melissa Koch stood up. The soft, rain-soaked dirt started giving way under her weight. She looked at me with fear in her eyes.

"Jump!" I yelled.

She placed her weight on her left foot as if to jump. The dirt at her feet crumbled and she slipped backward and fell again.

I started toward her. The dirt beneath my feet slid forward, almost taking me with it, and pushing Melissa Koch even further toward the vanishing cliff edge.

"For God's sake help me!" she screamed as gravity took her over.

I was trapped. Another step forward and I would join her. I removed my belt and got down on my belly.

"Grab my belt and hold on!" I said.

I could see my tee shirt and jogging shoes several hundred yards ahead. I pushed past the aches and burn, opened my stride as much as possible and went into a full-blown sprint.

My lungs burned for air.

Just her upper body was visible now as gravity worked its magic.

I stretched out and tossed the belt toward her. It fell about two feet short of the mark.

"You have to reach forward and grab it," I said.

Melissa Koch stared at the belt, paralyzed by fear.

"I . . . can't," she said.

"Yes you can," I said. "Grab the goddamn belt."

The dirt was crumbling quickly now. She sank under her own weight.

"Now! Do it now!" I shouted.

I saw her reach for the belt just as the soft dirt gave way completely. There was a split second of eye contact between us and then she was gone.

Just like that.

In the blink of an eye.

I raced the final thirty yards, collapsed to the sand and rolled over next to my tee shirt and shoes.

I sucked air and looked up at the blue sky dotted with milky white clouds.

Battery acid ran through my veins.

Bright sunlight peeked through the clouds and I closed my eyes.

For a moment I couldn't believe what I had just witnessed.

Slowly I stood up and stepped backward to the hiking path. The sky was light now, that first light of the new day was warm on my face.

It seemed forever ago that I stood on Koch's yacht where Melissa Koch gave me her warning. Watch your step, she said.

That was good advice.

She should have followed it.

When my breathing returned to normal I sat up, wrapped my arms around my knees and looked at the ocean.

The incident with Melissa Koch took place six weeks ago. A powerful senator's wife doesn't trip and fall to her death off a hundred-foot high cliff every day of the week, so it was major news. An accident heard around the world, so to speak.

For two weeks I was the guest of the Hawaiian State Police, known as Five-0 in popular culture. The FBI joined in on the fun. I was sliced and diced while they gathered evidence from the cliff where Melissa Koch did her swan dive and after many statements, written reports, reenactments, and the arrest of her lover and henchman, a slug of a man named Herb, they declared her death officially an accident.

Senator Oliver Koch left the Senate and flew to Hawaii the day after his wife's death, and put on his game face for the world of the media. Melissa Koch was buried in Hawaii for reasons unknown to me and then Koch flew back to Washington.

I was free to go home.

I didn't.

I wanted to, needed to, have a face-to-face sit down with Koch.

After the incident, my girlfriend, Janet, and daughter, Regan, wanted to fly to Hawaii, but there was nothing they could do. I told them to stay put. I needed some time before I returned.

Time to think.

Time to analyze what happened.

Time to accept that a woman was dead because I confronted her in the course of doing my job.

But mostly to ask myself if Melissa Koch's death was an accident or murder.

At the moment she ridiculed and threatened me, threatened Regan and Janet, I wanted that woman to vanish off the face of the Earth. Did she trip over my foot in a clumsy accident on her part, or because of my subconscious desire to retaliate?

In all honesty, I didn't know.

What I did know was that if in my heart I believed I murdered Melissa Koch, I would make one lousy husband and father and human being.

So I put off going home and leaned on my closest friend, Police Captain Walt Grimes, to track down Koch and tell him I wanted a meeting. To my surprise Koch agreed and told Walt he was planning a trip to his Hawaiian home after the Senate recessed for the summer. Word was that he would be flying in late tonight and would meet me at his home tomorrow afternoon.

For the past four weeks I'd called home every other night

and spoken with Regan and Janet. I told them I loved and missed them and they told me the same, but in the past couple weeks I detected a coldness in Janet's voice that I had never heard before.

Not quite anger, but definitely cold.

Could I blame her?

After I met with Koch I would grab the first available flight home and make it up to her and to Regan. I wasn't sure how, mostly by being the kind of man Janet needed in her life and the kind of father Regan deserved.

I put on my jogging shoes and carried the ankle weights off the beach to the string of white bungalows where I'd rented one for the month. They were small, a single bedroom with bath, a tiny kitchen, a backyard balcony with grill and the use of the fresh water pool.

I removed the key from the pocket in my shorts, let myself into Bungalow 21 and immediately put a pot of coffee to brew in the four-cup capacity coffeemaker. When it was done, I took a mug and a cigarette out to the balcony.

No one was in the pool.

By now the temperature was close to ninety, but Hawaii was an ocean kind of a place so the pool was rarely used by guests. Since most people have cell phones nowadays, the rooms were not equipped with a land-line phone. There were four pay phones on the grounds, but I never saw anyone use one.

That included me.

After consuming coffee and cigarette, I checked my cell phone for messages. There were none. With the time difference it was late afternoon or early evening back home so I wasn't expecting any.

I changed into swim trunks and walked to the pool. There was no need to step in to get acclimated to the water. The temperature was around eighty-six or so and I dove right in and swam the first lap underwater. A sixth the size of an Olympic pool, it required a lot of laps to equal a mile so I didn't count and just swam until I was tired.

As I did laps I allowed my mind to wander. That's not necessarily a good thing. Sometimes your thoughts wander into places you'd rather not go and stir up old hurts you'd rather not remember. I thought about all those wasted years spent drinking myself to sleep after my wife's murder and all those years of being an absentee father to a little girl who desperately needed a real one.

I don't drink anymore. Two plus years without a drop, but I can't get back the lost time. Nobody can.

I've traded one addiction for two others. I can't drink and don't, so I work out until the urge to open a bottle and pour a stiff one passes. I also need to work and keep myself busy. If I'm chasing after a whodunit, my thoughts and time are occupied with things other than my past failures and bourbon over ice. Janet wants me to retire my private investigator's license and get a nine-to-five so I can be home every night for dinner and TV, but that won't work for me. Janet and I love each other. People who love each other deal with each other's flaws and weaknesses as part of the better or worse package.

Somewhere around the fiftieth lap I came out of the pool. I grabbed a clean towel from a stack in a bin and swiped water off my body, and then went to my balcony.

The grill wasn't propane operated, but the old-fashioned coals and lighter fluid type. I had a bag of coals on the floor and added some to the used ones on the bottom of the grill. I squirted on some lighter fluid, struck a wooden match and tossed it in. The coals burst into flames.

It would take about twenty minutes for the flames to die down and the coals to turn gray, so I returned to the pool and used the shuffleboard court as a workout area. I got down and did push-ups. I started with my hands close to my shoulders and then spread them about four feet apart. I went back and forth between narrow and wide until my chest, shoulders and arms were on fire and then I took a few minutes' break. Then I did several sets of one-handed push-ups, alternating between left hand and right until I gave out and collapsed in a heap.

I rested just long enough to catch my breath and then did some ab work. Scissor situps, crunches, planks, leg raises. I did several sets of each until my stomach cramped and told me to stop.

I took a few minutes to recover and then jumped into the pool to rinse the sweat off and cool down. I floated around for a few minutes and when I climbed the ladder out and grabbed a towel, the young girl from the beach was standing beside the towel bin with her dog.

She was maybe twenty-one or two, blond and pretty. She wore a baseball cap and had her hair in a ponytail with the tail sticking out the back of the cap.

"Do you always kill yourself like this?" she said.

I rubbed the towel over my hair. "Pretty much, yeah."

"You need a haircut and shave," she said.

"I know."

"I smell a grill going."

"That's mine," I said. "I was just about to toss on some burgers."

"I'm Joey, Joey Fureal."

"Joey?"

"Josephine. My parents wanted a boy. They got me instead."

"Want a burger, Joey?"

"Sure. This is Buddy. Can he have one?"

"Why not?" I said. "Let me go put some clothes on. You and Buddy can wait on the balcony."

★　★　★　★　★

Joey bit into a burger and wiped juice off her chin with a napkin. "I followed you here from the beach," she said. "Actually it was Buddy who found you, but I asked him to."

"Why?"

"Curiosity mostly," Joey said. "You're that private investigator who threw the senator's wife off the cliff."

"That's one way of putting it."

"What's the other way?"

"She tripped and fell."

"That's what they said on the news."

At Joey's feet, Buddy licked the plate clean of the last bit of burger juice.

"They also said you were free to go home, so I was wondering, why are you still here?" Joey said.

"How old are you?" I said.

"Twenty-two," Joey said. "Almost. My birthday is next month."

"Remember first grade when your teacher gave you a time-out?" I said. "I'm taking a time-out."

"You're hiding," Joey said. "I live in the next mansion down from the senator. My dad is a hotshot lawyer and my mom is what you would call a socialite. That's a code word for boozer. I know when somebody is hiding something. What are you hiding from?"

"Are you always so direct with your elders?"

"I'm dying from stage one Hodgkins' lymphoma, so I don't have time to pitty-pat around," Joey said.

I just looked at her.

"Hey, it's all right," Joey said. "It is what it is and I'm not going down without a fight. In two weeks I'm going to Sloan Kettering for treatment, me and Buddy. I'll stay in a hospice so

Buddy can sleep in my room. He wouldn't leave my side anyway."

My appetite was gone, but I took a bite of my burger and washed it down with some coffee.

"So what are you hiding from?" Joey said.

"Myself."

"How does that work?"

When a kid tells you they're dying and then asks you a question, you answer it.

I started with when Regan was five years old and witnessed her mother's murder, covered the decade of drinking and recovery at the hands of mobster Eddie Crist, and ended with Melissa Koch on the cliff.

Joey listened and took it all in while eating a second burger. When I was done, so was she and she used another paper napkin to wipe her chin and fingers.

"Know what I think?" she said. "I think you're not the type to murder someone in cold blood, especially a woman. You're that old-fashioned type of guy who would let a woman beat him to death before he raised a hand to her."

"You base that on?" I said.

"Buddy likes you. Buddy is never wrong about people. If he sensed the slightest bit of bad in you he never would have allowed you to get this close to me."

I looked at Buddy. He looked at me like he wanted another burger. There was one left and I gave it to him.

"Feel like sitting by the ocean for a bit?" Joey said. "I've got nothing better to do and nobody to do it with."

"Why not?" I said. "Want something cold to drink?"

"Sure."

I grabbed a couple of cold sodas from the fridge, tucked my smokes in my shirt pocket and we walked the hundred yards or

so to the sand and took seats facing the waves as the tide started to roll out.

"So here's what's going to happen to me when I get to Sloan," Joey said as Buddy sat beside her and placed his head on her lap. "I'm going to receive chemotherapy every two weeks for several cycles and hope that it works. If it doesn't, then comes radiation therapy. Either way I'm going to feel sick all the time and will probably lose most of my hair. If it's necessary I'll have a bone marrow transplant from a relative or matched donor. I'm told they've done something like five thousand transplants of marrow at Sloan, but I'm hoping it won't come to that."

I opened my can of soda and washed some down, and then pulled out my cigarettes and lit one.

"You shouldn't smoke," Joey said.

"I know."

"It's really bad for you."

"I know."

"You exercise like some kind of freak on a sugar high and then light up a cigarette," Joey said. "That doesn't make sense."

"I know."

"I sound like an old nag, don't I?"

"You sound like my daughter and girlfriend," I said.

"Saying girlfriend sounds funny when you're . . ."

"What?"

"Being someone's girlfriend is usually reserved for someone under thirty."

"Then let's call her my lady friend."

"What does she call you?"

"Annoying."

Joey cracked a smile, opened her can of soda and took a sip. A few seconds of silence passed.

And then just like that the dam burst and she started to cry.

"Oh damn," Joey said in between sobs. "It's not fair . . . I just graduated college, for God's sake."

I stuck my cigarette in the sand and wrapped my arm around Joey's shoulder. "I know it's not fair," I said. "Very few things are."

"Listen to me," Joey said. "I sound like a spoiled brat, don't I?"

"You sound like a young woman who's afraid to die before she's had a chance to live. And that's perfectly normal for anybody."

Joey sniffled and sobbed for a bit longer and then regained control. She rubbed Buddy's ears and he responded by licking her fingers.

"I'm tired," she said. "I take two naps a day. I used to do gymnastics four hours a day and right now I can't even toss a Frisbee with Buddy."

"Right now," I said, "you have to believe that you will, or you won't. Sometimes failure is not an option."

Joey nodded and stood up. "Walk me home?"

"Sure."

Joey's home was a few hundred yards past the Koch mansion, a mile and a half down the beach. We didn't hurry. Buddy stayed by Joey's side even though I could see the young dog wanted to bust loose and run.

"I'm scared, you know," Joey confessed, "of having to go to Sloan for treatment and of what happens if the treatment fails."

"When the time comes you won't be afraid," I said.

"How do you know?"

"Back when I was a cop there wasn't a day I didn't think today could be the day I have to draw my gun and today could be the day I die of a bullet from a crazed criminal," I said. "And then you leave the house and go do your job, and if and when the time comes you do have to pull your weapon, those thoughts go away and you do what you have to. That's what will happen to you. You'll be afraid right up until the time you have to do what you have to do, and then you won't be afraid at all."

Joey looked at me. "Promise?"

"Yes."

We arrived at the five-hundred-step wooden staircase that went from the beach to Joey's home on the cliff. We were so engaged in conversation that I didn't realize we'd strolled right past the Koch mansion. The handrail had a motorized chair on it.

"My dad had that put in a few years ago for my mom," Joey said. "He worries she'll trip and fall after happy hour. I never used it until recently."

Joey took the chair and Buddy jumped on her lap.

"Hold on, boy. We go for a ride now," Joey said and pushed a button.

The chair slowly ascended the stairs. When it was around twenty feet high, Joey said, "Hey, meet me on the beach tomorrow. I'll bring Buddy's Frisbee."

"After I see Koch, come by the bungalow," I said.

Joey took hold of Buddy's front paw and waved to me. "Bye-bye," she said.

I returned to my bungalow, sat on the balcony, drank coffee and smoked a few butts.

Joey made me long for Regan.

I grabbed my cell phone and punched in the number for Janet's home, where Regan was staying.

"Dad?" Regan said. "Is something wrong? Are you coming home?"

"No and yes," I said.

"When?"

"Two days at the most. I have to book a flight. I'll let you know the number and time. Everything okay on your end?"

"Mark decided to take summer school classes," Regan said. "I'm helping him with homework. Oz is in the kitchen cooking something."

"Oz?" I said. "Where's Janet?"

"Working a double shift at the hospital," Regan said. "She's going to Chicago for a month day after tomorrow and wanted to catch up on paperwork."

"Chicago? What for?"

"She's getting a promotion at the hospital," Regan said. "She's going for some kind of training to run the post-op ward."

"Ask her to call me when she gets in."

"It will be late."

"Not here it won't."

"That's right. Okay, I'll tell her."

We chatted for a bit and when I hung up I felt very alone and lonely for my family.

Even for Oz.

Sometimes trying to do the right thing is a lonely business.

At least it was for me.

TWO

It bothered me a bit in the morning that Janet hadn't returned my call, but she probably got in late and was tired and had to pack for her trip to the Windy City, and it slipped her mind.

I occupied my thoughts with what I was going to say to Senator Koch. It's not like you can walk up to someone after causing his wife to trip and fall off a hundred-foot high cliff and say, "Oops, my bad," and that would be the end of it.

I shaved, showered and then put on the lightweight suit I'd worn the morning I confronted Melissa Koch. I hadn't brought a lot of clothing with me to Hawaii as I wasn't planning on more than an overnight stay, though I was allowed to buy what I needed while being held for questioning.

I skipped breakfast and settled for three cups of coffee and an equal number of cigarettes. It wasn't exactly the breakfast of champions, but I lacked an appetite and there was no sense fixing something I wouldn't eat.

I walked the mile and a half from the bungalow to the Koch mansion. The tall iron gates were open when I arrived. As a senator Koch wasn't entitled to Secret Service protection, but he could well afford a private army of his own.

Two men were on duty in the guardhouse. One came out to greet me as I strolled though the open gates. I gave him my name and he said, "The Senator is having lunch in the backyard. He told me to ride you up when you arrived."

Ride me up meant a trip from the gate to the backyard gardens in a golf cart. As the distance was several acres and I was sweated through to my shirt already, I didn't mind riding shotgun.

Senator Koch was waiting for me, drinking coffee at a patio table. He was dressed in comfortable clothing suited for Hawaii and appeared rested and relaxed. He stood and filled a cup for me, then waited for me to settle into a chair before he sat back down.

"I'm retiring from the Senate," Koch said. "From public life altogether. I never wanted to be a senator or run for the VP nod; that was all my wife. She had a push-push, drive-at-all-cost mentality and I went along with her for thirty-plus years. She murdered a young woman because I had an affair with her and then murdered my assistant to cover up her deeds. Melissa was an evil woman, Bekker, interested only in her own rise to fame and power, and I am not in the least bit saddened by her death. For the first time in thirty years I feel free and alive, and I plan to enjoy what remaining years I have left. So, what's on your mind this fine beautiful morning that you so want to share with me?"

"My conscience is bothering me," I said.

Koch set his coffee cup down and eyed me. "Your conscience?" he said. "Why?"

"Because I'm not sure if her trip and fall was entirely an accident," I said. "I tried to save her at the risk of going over myself, but in my mind I'm not sure if I caused her to trip in the first place. She threatened me and my family, and when she walked past me and tripped over my foot, I may have wanted her to. Maybe not to kill her, but to humiliate her. I just wanted to tell you that."

Koch sipped a bit more coffee as he studied me. "Bekker, I really don't care about your conscience," he said as he set the cup down again. "She got exactly what she deserved and that's called justice. I can tell you, based upon what I know of you, that I don't believe you're capable of outright murder. For what that's worth, that's what I believe. You believe what you want."

"For what it's worth, thank you," I said.

"Would you like some lunch?"

"Sure."

We ate a three-course lunch prepared by Koch's chef and chatted for ninety minutes. He told me some war stories about the Senate and I told him some war stories about being a cop.

Then we shook hands and he offered to have one of his men drive me back to the bungalow. "A full stomach, ninety-one degrees, a mile-walk isn't a good combination for the digestion," he said.

Joey and Buddy were waiting for me poolside when Koch's driver dropped me off at the bungalows. Buddy had a red Frisbee in his mouth.

"You made it out alive," Joey said when I walked to her.

"I did," I said. "Give me a minute to ditch this monkey suit."

I went in through the balcony door and changed into shorts, tank top and sneakers. I filled a cooler with ice and soda, tucked my smokes into a pocket and did a quick check of my cell phone for messages.

There weren't any.

"So are you off the hook?" Joey said as I carried the cooler down to the beach.

"With Koch?"

"Yourself."

"Let's just say I'm leaning in that direction."

"So you'll be going home?"

"Tomorrow if I can book a flight."

We arrived at the beach. I set the cooler down away from the waves.

"I don't have the energy to run much, but Buddy does most of the work," Joey said as she took the Frisbee from Buddy.

I walked about a hundred feet down the beach and faced Joey. Buddy kind of just stood in the middle and waited for Joey to toss the Frisbee to me. Buddy's idea of a good time was for us to toss the Frisbee to each other and for him to try to intercept it midflight.

Buddy was successful about fifty percent of the time.

After about an hour Buddy needed a break from the heat and took a quick dip in the ocean. Joey and I sat by the cooler and drank sodas and when Buddy emerged from the water, I gave him some ice cubes to chomp on.

"I thought about what you said yesterday," Joey said. "About being afraid."

I pulled out my cigarettes and lit one.

"I'm not sure I'm strong enough," Joey said. "I'm scared. Really scared."

"That's good," I said. "Being scared is what makes you a good driver. Being scared is what makes you a good cop. Being scared of losing something means you care about it and when you care about it you're willing to fight to keep it. Being scared is what gives you courage. You can't be brave if you aren't afraid. They go hand in hand."

"Did you teach that to your daughter?"

"More like the other way around."

"I'll think that one over," Joey said.

Buddy had the Frisbee in his mouth again.

"I think he's ready for round two," I said.

Around five in the afternoon I walked a very tired Joey and Buddy to the stairs that led to her home in the cliffs.

"Will you come say good-bye to me before you leave?" Joey said as she and Buddy took the seat.

"I will."

Joey hit the lever and the chair began to ascend.

"I'll hunt you down if you don't," she said.

The first thing I did when I returned to the bungalow was check for messages. Still none. I made some coffee and took a cup and my cell phone to a chair by the pool, lit up a cigarette.

While I was debating whether to call Janet or hold off, the cell phone rang. I checked the incoming number. It was Janet and I scooped it up.

"Hi, I was just arguing with myself if I should call or wait a bit," I said.

"Regan told me you're coming home," Janet said.

"Tomorrow if I can."

"So what did you accomplish by staying an extra month?" Janet's voice was cold, almost callous.

"I can't explain on the phone," I said. "I'll explain when I get home tomorrow."

"This time tomorrow I will be in Chicago," Janet said. "I've made arrangements for Mark to stay with Clayton while I'm away and for Oz to stay at my house with Regan until you get back."

"Look, I don't blame you for being angry, but I can . . ."

"I'm not angry," Janet said. "The hospital promoted me to supervisor of the ICU recovery ward. They're sending me to Chicago for a month of training. I have a great deal on my mind and much to learn. There are other things in life besides the adventures of the great John Bekker, you know."

I wouldn't say I was stunned, as I had that coming, but to hear such harsh words from Janet and in such a cold, dry tone gave me serious pause.

"Okay, I deserved that, but at least allow me to explain why I stayed in Hawaii," I said. "I could come to Chicago and we could . . ."

"Jack, I have some serious work to do and not much time to learn what I need to learn," Janet said. "Don't come to Chicago. I can't afford to get sidetracked with this. We'll talk when I come home."

"Even for a weekend or just a day?"

"It's not the time, it's the distraction it will cause me," Janet said. "I'm expected to learn and then be able to teach life and death procedures to the nurses on my staff. If I'm preoccupied with thoughts of you and the fantasy world you live in I may not return to the hospital with one hundred percent of what I need to know."

"Fantasy world?" I said. "What the hell are you talking about? Melissa Koch died because I confronted her on the cliff on the Koch property, and if I need to remind you, it was at your asking that I even took the job in the first place."

"And I felt very guilty about that," Janet said. "But when I wanted you to come home and you wanted to stay and I wanted to come there to be with you, you pushed me away. And maybe it's selfish of me, but I don't feel guilty about it anymore. Now we'll talk when I get home in a month and that's all I'm going to say about it."

"I didn't push you away," I said. "I needed some time alone to come to grips with what happened."

"And did you?"

"I think so," I said. "That's why I'm going home tomorrow."

"Good," Janet said. "Regan needs you."

"And you?"

"I never needed you, Jack," Janet said. "A healthy relationship is based upon want, not need. I wanted you and there is a difference between the two. We'll talk about all this when I get back and we've both had time to evaluate things. Fair?"

"Okay," I said. "Just let me say this. I still love you very much and I'm willing to do whatever it takes to make this work."

"I know that," Janet said. "And I love you too, Jack. Now I have to go and finish packing."

I said good-bye, hung up, and sat there with cold coffee and a fresh cigarette. I drank the coffee while I called the airlines and made a reservation for a flight that left at noon and got me home around nine at night.

I didn't want to think about how mad Janet was at me, so I decided to burn off my anxiety with a workout. I went for a long run on the beach and watched the sun slowly set over the ocean, and then exhausted every muscle in my body with push-ups, situps and some laps in the pool. I was on empty, emotionally and physically, by the time I found my way into my bungalow to take a hot shower.

There was still plenty of food in the fridge and cupboards. I put on some spaghetti and meatballs with garlic bread and busied myself at the table with a few cigarettes.

That's when I noticed a message on the cell phone I'd missed earlier.

My close friend and frequent colleague, Sheriff Jane Morgan.

I did a quick guesstimate of the time zones and decided she would be asleep for several more hours, so I called and left a message on her voicemail.

I ate my late-night supper while watching a rerun of, what else, *Hawaii-50* and then called it a night and tucked myself into bed.

Three hours later my cell phone ringing woke me up. It was Jane returning my message. "Bekker, you awake?"

I glanced at the digital alarm clock beside the bed. It was three in the morning.

"I am now," I said.

"Sorry about the time thing, but I talked to Regan yesterday and she said you're coming home," Jane said. "I need a favor."

"Jane, Janet all but dumped me over . . ."

"Janet's gone bye-bye to Chicago for a month," Jane said. "Regan told me."

"What favor?"

"When can we meet?"

"It's that important?"

"I'm calling you at three in the morning, aren't I?" Jane said.

"I'll be in around nine tomorrow night," I said. "First thing in the morning stop by the trailer."

"Night-night, Bekker," Jane said.

"Yeah."

THREE

Since the bungalows were just a mile from town I hadn't bothered with a rental car, but the airport was too far to walk so I reserved a taxi.

The drivers work on speed, on how many round-trips to the airport they can make in a given shift, so when you ask a driver to wait for an extended period of time they generally have a hissy fit. I told the driver I would add a fifty-dollar bill to the meter if he took me to the Fureal mansion and gave me a ten-minute wait.

As soon as the cab pulled up to the house Joey and Buddy came out to greet me. Joey wore cutoff shorts and a white tank top. Buddy wore his golden fur.

Joey gave me a hug.

Buddy gave me a hand lick.

"I'm off," I said.

"Me, too, in another ten days or less," Joey said.

I dipped into my suit-jacket pocket for my business card and placed it in Joey's hand. "If you feel like talking one day, give me a call," I said.

"Thanks," Joey said. "I will."

I scratched Buddy's ears. "You'll be fine," I said. "They know what they're doing at Sloan. And don't be afraid of being afraid. Remember what I told you."

Joey nodded, showed me a smile and gave me another hug.

As I walked back to the cab, she called after me. "You look

31

good clean shaven," she said. "Still need a haircut, though."

I opened the door to the cab and smiled at Joey.

"And a new suit," she added.

When I walked through the gate around nine-thirty in the evening, I spotted Regan and Oz waiting for me on the other side.

"Dad!" Regan shouted and ran to me. She jumped into my arms the way an eight-year-old would and a nineteen-year-old normally wouldn't.

I didn't mind one bit.

"Gained some weight," I told her. "Must be up to a hundred pounds by now."

After I set Regan down she took my hand and we met Oz and walked down the stairs to baggage claim.

"You bring me a bottle of them nuts they got there?" Oz said.

"What nuts?" I said.

"Them Hawaiian nuts they grow only in Hawaii, them nuts."

"Macadamia?" I said. "They sell them in any grocery store."

"I know," Oz said. "It's the thought what counts."

"I did bring you a nifty shirt," I said.

"Terrific," Oz said.

"And something for you," I said as I kissed Regan's nose.

"What?" Regan said with childlike innocence.

"It's in my luggage," I said. "Can you wait until we get home?"

Regan nodded, but I could see the excitement in her eyes.

"Keep an eye out for my luggage while I reserve a cab," I said.

"No need," Oz said. "I drove your crap mobile."

"My car isn't that bad," I said.

"Dad, it's as old as I am," Regan said.

"It's a classic," I said.

"A 1956 cherry-red Thunderbird is a classic," Oz said. "What you drive is otherwise known as junk. I see your bags."

Oz drove. I sat beside him and Regan behind me. After about a mile I noticed Oz didn't take the road to Janet's house but to the beach.

"This is the way to the beach," I said.

Oz glanced at me. "Is there no end to your detective skills," he said. "Ain't that right, girl?"

"Almost like a super power," Regan said.

"Funny," I said and patted my pockets.

"Dad, do you smell that?" Regan said.

"What? I don't smell anything."

"That nothing you smell is a lack of cigarette butts, ashes and smoke," Regan said. "I cleaned and washed every square inch of this car and if you think you're lighting up in here I'll bite you on the back of the neck. Is that clear?"

"Yes ma'am," I said.

Oz grinned at me ear to ear.

"You shut up," I told him.

The floodlight was on when we arrived at my trailer. What greeted me were four new beach chairs, an actual patio table and a spanking new stainless-steel barbeque grill.

"Wait till you see inside," Regan said with the excitement of a kid on Christmas morning when she knew she'd scored the gift she really wanted.

The trailer was neat as a pin. My bedroom, the guest bedroom, bathroom, shower, kitchen and what passed for a living room.

"How long did this take you?" I said.

"A week," Regan said. "Me and Oz did it. When Aunt Janet told me she had to go to Chicago last week I decided I'd rather stay here at the beach."

"Hungry?" Oz said.

"A bit."

"Good. I been itching to try out the new grill."

"I'm stuffed," I said after consuming three burgers, two dogs and a plate of fries. "And now for gifts."

I went inside for a moment to dig out the shirt for Oz and the small box I picked up for Regan at the duty-free jewelry store inside the airport.

Oz held the bright yellow shirt decorated with pineapples and palm trees to the floodlight and nodded.

"Ain't as bad as I thought it'd be," Oz said. "At night. In the dark. If I squint."

I held the small gift-wrapped box out to Regan.

She took it and looked at me. "What's in it?"

"Only one way to find out," I said.

Regan slowly removed the silver paper, opened the lid and looked at the one-karat diamond earrings inside.

"Dad . . ."

"You're a grownup girl, you should have some grownup earrings," I said.

My grownup girl removed the earrings from the box and started to sniffle. "Can I try them on?"

"They're yours," I said.

Regan pinned an earring to each ear and did a spin for us. "How do they look?"

"Like a movie star," Oz said.

Regan gave me a tight hug. Her face barely came to my chest.

"Why am I so short?" she said.

"Because good things come in small packages," I said. "Now if Oz will take his beautiful new shirt and go home, the jet lag is killing me and I'd like to get some sleep."

"Just for buying me this shirt I'm going to wear it in the daytime and make you look at it," Oz said.

FOUR

I opened my eyes when I heard Regan's voice through the open window of my bedroom.

"My dad's asleep," she said. "Jet lag."

"He's expecting me," Jane said. "We talked on the phone yesterday."

"He's retired from investigating," Regan said.

"I know, hon, but this is important," Jane said. "Otherwise I wouldn't ask."

I heard Regan sigh loudly.

"I'll get him," she said. "I was going to get him up anyway. Have some coffee. I just made it."

I stumbled from the bed to the bathroom and ran the water in the sink.

"Dad, that sheriff is here," Regan called out to me.

"I heard," I said. "I'll be right out."

I let the sink fill with cold water and stuck my face in it for thirty seconds. Then I brushed my teeth and ran a brush through my shaggy hair.

Jane and Regan were in the new chairs at the new patio table when I emerged from the trailer. "I like what you've done with the place," Jane said.

"Regan and Oz did it while I was away." I filled a mug with coffee and took a seat.

"Want some breakfast?" Regan said.

"In a bit."

"I hate to ask, Bekker, but I need help," Jane said.

Regan glared at Jane. "Should I leave?"

"You can stay," I said.

"It's pretty gruesome, Bekker," Jane said.

I looked at Regan. "I'll stay," she said.

"Okay," Jane said.

I looked around the table for my cigarettes.

"I tossed them," Regan said.

I looked at her.

"The extra packs in your luggage, too."

I nodded. "So what's the emergency?" I said to Jane.

"I have a total staff of ninety deputies to man the entire county and jail," Jane said. "I'm lucky I can put two cruisers on the street 24-7. I have one vacancy in my three-man detective squad and the other two are out of their league on this. I tried to borrow a detective or two from Walt, but he's swamped. I asked the county comptroller for special funds to pay your fee and they agreed. Mostly because it's bad for the tourist season and they don't want this to linger on to fall when the second round shows up to gawk at the leaves and all the pretty colors."

I sipped some coffee and looked around the table again for my smokes.

"They're gone, Dad," Regan said. "Get over it."

"What is bad for tourist season?" I said to Jane.

"Are you familiar with Midnight Island?" Jane said.

Midnight Island is three miles off the coast. About four miles long, a mile and a half at its widest point, it's home to about nine hundred year-round residents. That number swells to three thousand during the summer months. A ferry makes eight round trips to the mainland daily and four on Sunday.

"I've been there once or twice," I said. "A long time ago. I had lunch with Carol at this old hotel restaurant."

"The kid from the high school," Regan said. "That's what

this is about, isn't it?"

Jane nodded.

"What kid?" I said.

"Bekker, we should really bring this to my office," Jane said.

"Oz is coming," Regan said.

Wearing the bright yellow shirt, Oz strolled from his trailer to mine.

"What are you supposed to be?" Jane said when Oz arrived.

"Ask Bekker, it's his shirt," Oz said.

"Want some breakfast?" Regan said to Oz as he took a chair.

"Let's all have some breakfast," I said. "Then I'll get dressed and go to the office with Jane. Oz, you hang around. Okay?"

"Where I gonna go looking like Tweety Bird?" Oz said.

I rode with Jane in her cruiser and left Oz the keys to my car. After checking me in as a guest at the desk, we went to her office. She called the dispatcher and asked to have her calls held.

"Want some coffee first?" Jane said.

"Sure."

Jane called somebody on her phone and a female deputy showed up with two containers of coffee from the break room.

"You need to see this," Jane said as she removed a DVD from a desk drawer and inserted it into the player where it rested on top of a television to the right of her desk. With a remote, Jane turned on the monitor and hit the play button.

"Deputy Spears arrived on scene first, closely followed by Deputy Andrews," Jane said. "They activated their mounted cameras on their cruisers and mini-cams on their uniforms immediately upon arrival at the County Regional High School. This shot came from a mini-cam."

The monitor brightened as the high school came into view. The recording time in the right-hand corner was 2:33 in the afternoon.

"There!" I heard a deputy shout.

In the background, a man screamed, "Motherfucker, I'll kill you!"

The POV of the mini-cam showed the deputies rushing around a fence onto the football field.

"Freeze!" a deputy screamed.

"That's Spears," Jane said.

"Put down the fucking bat!" another deputy screamed. "Put it down now!"

"That's Andrews," Jane said.

The angle of the POV shifted again and a large man with a baseball bat was beating a kid on the ground in the head and face with it.

"Motherfucker!" the man screamed.

"That is Mr. Norman Felton, a resident of Midnight Island," Jane said.

"Down, down, put down the bat and put your hands on your head!" Andrews yelled. "Now!"

Felton turned and looked at the deputies. His face was a mask of insane fury. He raised the bat and charged the deputies. There was a loud thud followed by a gunshot.

As Felton fell from view, Andrews yelled, "Fuck. You shot him! Fuck!"

"He broke my arm," Spears said.

The POV shifted again and Felton was on the grass, bleeding from a gunshot to the head. Next to Felton, a teenage boy was unconscious, beaten to a pulp.

Jane hit the pause button.

"Deputy Spears suffered a broken forearm when Mr. Felton hit him with the bat," she said. "The mini-cam shows the shooting was clearly accidental and caused by the bat striking Spears on the left arm. The gun went off on impact. The kid is Ubaldo Montero, an eighteen-year-old exchange student from the

Dominican Republic. His father has applied for an emergency visa to come to the States. It hasn't gone through as yet, but it should within a few days."

I pulled out my cigarettes, lit two and gave Jane one.

"Felton?" I said.

"In county prison hospital in a coma," Jane said.

"The Montero kid?"

"Three floors below in the coma ward."

"So what do we know?" I said.

"We know that Mr. Felton caught the ferry at one in the afternoon and drove straight to the high school," Jane said. "We know he assaulted Ubaldo Montero on the football field, where Montero volunteers as a groundskeeper for the school and was touching up the field when Felton attacked. We know that a school official working on Saturday looked out her window when she heard Felton screaming and called 911. We don't know motive, but I would bet the farm it's about Felton's missing fourteen-year-old daughter, Amanda."

"Missing?" I said. "For how long?"

"The day of the incident is our best guess," Jane said. "We have no leads or witnesses on the island who can tell us otherwise. I entered her into the FBI databank, put out an alert to all police and sheriff departments in the county, and established an 800 hotline for information. Nada with a capital N."

"And who besides us wants her back?" I said.

"That would be Robert Felton, older brother of Norman Felton," Jane said. "He resides in Rhode Island. I told him I would be bringing in a consultant to assist me. He said he will pay your going rate with a bonus if you find Amanda alive. I checked with county lawyers and there is no law against you taking this case unless you withhold evidence or act in a criminal manner."

"I thought you said the county agreed to my fees?" I said.

"I told Felton that he couldn't hire you, as you would be working as an advisor to the Sheriff's Department," Jane said.

"What if I turned you down?" I said.

Jane gave me her look that said, *That would be a first.*

I shrugged and sipped coffee. "What does the county consider a criminal matter?"

Jane opened her desk drawer and pulled out a pack of smokes. She gave me one and we both lit up.

"Smoking in a public building would be a criminal matter," she said as she flared her nostrils and blew out smoke.

"Okay, I'm in," I said. "Give me whatever agreement document you have and I'll get started. God knows I have nothing better to occupy my time."

Jane nodded. "What do you need from me?"

"Besides that we work together on this, the evidence log, a copy of this DVD, statements from the witness, hospital reports, a meeting with the arresting officers, reports on the Felton home inspection, a list of his friends, family and the daughter's friends on the island and at school," I said. "For starters."

Jane looked at me.

"And your gut instinct," I said.

"The only thing my gut has is about two inches too much around the middle," Jane said. "There's no visible connection between the girl, who is in the eighth grade and enrolled at the middle school four miles from the high school, and the Montero boy, a senior at the high school."

"Where does he live?" I said.

"In town with his exchange-student foster parents."

"Add them to my list."

"Anything else?"

"Tomorrow morning, call both schools and tell them I'll be stopping by to do some research," I said. "Make it after lunch so I have time in the morning to review your list."

"Okay," Jane said. "I'll drive you back and then put your list together."

In the cruiser on the way back, Jane fired up two cigarettes and gave me one.

"I don't mean to meddle, Bekker, but I heard from Regan about Janet going to Chicago for a month," she said. "I got the impression Janet isn't too happy with you right now."

"I can't blame her for that," I said.

"Why did you stay that extra month?"

"Work on my conscience," I said.

Jane nodded. "A conscience has a way of screwing things up," she said. "But in the end things always work out one way or another."

"I know," I said.

A lifetime ago when I was a kid in Bible study class, I asked the priest teaching the class why God didn't answer my prayer to make my grandmother better and let her live. He told me God did answer my prayer, but that sometimes the answer is no.

Things working out are a lot like prayer in that regard.

FIVE

After Jane dropped me off I decided to go for a run since my car, Oz and Regan were gone.

I changed into shorts, tee shirt and running shoes. I stretched for a bit and then jogged slowly down to the beach. The tide was up and surfers in black wetsuits dotted the landscape.

I ran for thirty minutes before removing my shirt and tucking it into my shorts and turning around. On the way back I upped my pace and my mind entered the zone of quiet. Thoughts are shut out and all you hear is your own heartbeat and rhythmic breathing. Runner's high, they call it. I call it peace and quiet.

Not true.

I call it escape.

Regan was at the patio table waiting for me when I returned.

My daughter knows her father. A fresh pot of coffee was on the table beside her. A towel hung over a vacant chair.

I arrived at the table, grabbed the towel and wiped my face before taking a chair. "Where did you and Oz disappear to?" I said.

"I asked him to take me to that tobacco store on Elm Street," Regan said. "And to pick up Molly from Aunt Janet's house."

My hopes were up as I filled a mug with coffee.

"I bought you this," Regan said. She produced a gift-wrapped box from her lap and set it on the table.

Before I could reach for the box, Molly magically appeared

from somewhere and jumped onto Regan's lap.

I removed the wrapper from the box to reveal a complete kit for electronic cigarettes.

"I know you tried them a few years ago, but they've improved them now and I want you to try them again," Regan said. "And also wear sunblock when you go running around shirtless in the sun. There is a thing called skin cancer you should know about. Okay?"

I nodded.

"Uncle Walt called," Regan said. "He's stopping by. I told him I would make us all lunch, so you sit and try one of those cigarettes, drink your coffee, and I'll make something to eat."

"Yes, ma'am," I said.

Molly followed Regan into the kitchen.

I looked at the electronic cigarette kit and finally opened it. The starter kit held two ceramic filters, four screw-on white tubes and a battery charger. The instructions said the filters were fully charged and ready to go. One white tube was equal to two packs of cigarettes. Five puffs on one tube were equal to one regular cigarette.

I screwed a tube to the filter. It was about the length of a king-size filtered cigarette.

I sighed and placed it between my lips.

From behind me, Regan said, "I see Uncle Walt's car."

Walt's unmarked sedan was headed our way across the beach.

I took a puff on the electronic cigarette and the tip glowed red. It wasn't as bad as I thought it would be, but not as good as the real thing. Most things in life aren't.

Walt arrived, parked and exited his sedan wearing a charcoal gray, lightweight suit with white shirt and paisley tie.

Regan gave Walt a warm hug and kiss on the cheek. "Lunch is almost ready," she said. "So you two have some guy talk time."

Walt looked around. "Where's the cat?"

"Wherever Regan is."

"So as your best bud maybe you could enlighten me as to why you stayed in Hawaii so long?" Walt said.

"Work on my conscience, wait for Koch to show up, come to grips with killing Melissa Koch," I said.

"I read all the PD reports," Walt said. "It was an accident. Even the Senator said so in a statement."

"Say you were driving home one dark night and just didn't see a kid on a tricycle as he darted out from the curb," I said. "It was an accident you ran him over, but wouldn't you feel just as guilty as if it weren't?"

Walt sighed. "What the hell are you smoking?"

"A gift from my daughter," I said.

"And your lady?"

"She's in school in Chicago for a month," I said. "And she's not too happy with me right now."

"Do you blame her?"

"No."

I took another hit on the e-cigarette.

"How are those things?" Walt said.

"Like food without salt," I said.

Walt nodded. "You gonna help Jane? She wanted to borrow a detective, but I'm short-handed as it is and the mayor would never go for it."

"I met with her this morning," I said. "Any ideas?"

"I haven't looked at any evidence or read statements," Walt said. "But Norman Felton was obviously in a rage over something and I'd guess it's his missing daughter. Without Felton telling us why he attacked that kid it's the only obvious link."

"About as I see it," I said.

"I'll help when I can," Walt said.

"Enough boy talk," Regan said as she emerged from the trailer with a large serving tray loaded down with thick club sandwiches, pickles, chips, fries and bottles of cold soda.

"Where is the . . . ?" Walt said as Molly jumped onto the table.

"I called Oz," Regan said as she looked at me. "Okay?"

"Did you ask him to change his shirt?"

"No."

"Why does he need to change his shirt?" Walt said.

"That's why," I said and pointed to Oz as he merrily strolled toward us in his canary yellow shirt.

After Walt returned to work, Oz and I sipped coffee while Regan cleaned up in the kitchen.

I waited for her to join us at the table before I said, "Oz, I'd like you to do me a favor."

About to sip coffee, Oz paused and gave me his look. "Is it one of your favors where people shoot at me?" he said.

"I doubt it," I said.

"Try to beat me up?"

"Probably not."

"Will I get paid?"

"In free burgers and hot dogs."

"In that case, what is it?"

"I'd like you to teach Regan to drive," I said.

Regan shot her gaze in my direction.

"Me?" Oz said.

"You're a good driver and I'm a lousy teacher," I said. "I would screw it up and I think it's about time Regan got her license. What do you think?"

"Do I get a car?" Regan said.

"If you get a license you can have mine," I said.

"A car that wasn't first owned by Fred Flintstone," Regan

said. "Or smells like the city dump."

"Take it or leave it," I said.

Regan looked at Oz.

He nodded at her.

"Yabba dabba doo," Regan said.

Six

While Oz drove Regan to the motor vehicle bureau to get a learner's permit, I called Jane and she picked me up in her cruiser.

"Have breakfast yet?" I said as I slid into the passenger seat.

"No."

"Let's pick up some on the way in," I said.

Jane hit the drive-through for egg sandwiches with hash browns and coffee. I carried the bags to her office where I broke out the food while she set up the DVD player.

We watched the incident for the second time, then a third. As far as I could determine from viewing it, Deputy Spears and Deputy Andrews followed procedure one hundred percent by the book and the shooting was completely accidental.

It was difficult to determine if Felton meant to attack the deputies or was so insane with fury that he didn't know what he was doing. It appeared he was out of control when he struck Spears with the baseball bat.

It was in his eyes. That look that said *occupant missing in action, please check back later when I'm home again.*

Question was, why?

What could drive an otherwise sane man to get in his car, ferry it to town and beat a kid half to death with a Louisville Slugger?

Did the Montero kid have something to do with Amanda Felton's disappearance?

Did Amanda run away from home and did Normal Felton blame the Montero kid for it? If so, why?

On the surface the fourteen-year-old girl and eighteen-year-old boy weren't connected in any way.

On the surface.

On the surface the iceberg that sunk the Titanic didn't appear all that much, either.

"Any sign of the Felton girl yet?" I said.

Jane shook her head as she finished off a hash brown.

"Have a contact number for the brother, what's his name?"

"Robert," Jane said. "Robert Felton. Owns a car dealership." She gave me the number and I punched it into my cell phone.

"Good morning, Felton Motors, how may I direct your call?" a chipper female voice said.

"John Bekker calling for Mr. Felton," I said. "I'm a special investigator with the Sheriff's Department."

"Please hold."

I held. And listened to Kenny G for sixty seconds or so. Finally Kenny G shut up and Robert Felton came on the line.

"I had to think a minute before it hit me," Felton said. "The investigator recommended by that woman sheriff, right?"

"I'm assisting the sheriff with the investigation," I said. "I'd like to talk to you about it as soon as possible."

"I'm in Rhode Island," Felton said.

"Not a problem. Tomorrow mid-afternoon okay?"

"Yeah, sure, I guess so," Felton said.

"Need directions?"

"I'll manage."

I hung up and looked at Jane.

"Want some fresh coffee?" she said.

"Sure."

While Jane left her office I scribbled some notes on a pad on her desk. *Are the DVD's available from the POV from the patrol cars? Besides the teacher in the school were there any others on the field or within view of the attack? Was the teacher's the only 911 call to the high school?*

Jane returned with two containers from the break room.

"Can you play the 911 call?" I said.

Jane went behind her desk and pulled a small recorder from a drawer.

Before she hit the play button, I removed the electronic cigarette from a pocket and stuck it between my lips. Jane looked at it.

"A gift from Regan," I said.

"How are they?" Jane said. "Better than last time?"

"Like taking your sister to the prom," I said.

Jane nodded and hit play.

"911, what's your emergency please?"

"I'm at the regional high school and there's a man beating up what looks like a teenage boy with a baseball bat."

"Are you inside the school?"

"Yes. Third floor."

"Are you sure the man is hitting the teenage boy with a bat?"

"Of course I'm sure. I'm watching him. The boy is against the fence and . . . oh, he just went down."

"Sheriff's deputies are on the way. Please stay inside. What is your name?"

"Sheryl Johnson. I'm a teacher here at the school."

"Stay on the line until the deputies arrive."

"Okay."

"Play it back," I said.

We listened to the call three more times. I made another note on the pad. *How long was the response time from when the call was placed to the deputies' arrival?*

I sucked on the electronic cigarette and exhaled water vapor.

"Can I try that?" Jane said.

I gave her the cigarette. She inhaled and blew out vapor. "It's close," she said. "But no cigar."

"Where's the evidence log?" I said.

Jane passed me the log book. It was open to the Felton page.

One standard, 32-ounce Louisville Slugger baseball bat made of maple wood and available anywhere sporting goods were sold. Blood on the bat matched blood from Ubaldo Montero. Hair on the bat came from the head of Ubaldo Montero. Blood on Normal Felton's clothing and skin matched blood from Ubaldo Montero.

The 911 call made by the teacher, Sheryl Johnson, and her written statement.

The DVD recording made by deputies Spears and Andrews and their written statements.

Hospital reports of the injuries to Ubaldo Montero. Hospital reports of the gunshot wound to Norman Felton. Hospital reports of Deputy Spears's broken right arm caused by Felton's attack with the baseball bat.

I read the reports filed by Deputy Spears and Deputy Andrews.

I read the initial and follow-up reports from Detective Philip Eaton and Detective Stan Hollis.

"What do you got on Normal Felton?" I said.

Jane handed me a file.

Norman Felton. Age forty-four. Graduated high school and attended college for two years. Took a job with the Post Office where he's been employed for twenty-three years, first as a loader, then sorter and finally to delivery. His tax returns for the previous year listed as income a total of sixty-three thousand with some modest capital gains on investments. His pension was fully vested and would have made his retirement at age fifty-five very comfortable.

His present duty station was on the mainland with scheduled

hours between six-thirty in the morning until two-thirty in the afternoon. That meant a five-thirty in the morning ferry ride five days a week.

During his second year at the post office, Felton met Susan Wiggs, a sorter at the mainland station he was assigned to. A romance blossomed and marriage soon followed. They put off having children until they could afford to purchase a home and when they could, they found a modest, Tudor-style home on Midnight Island.

Susan transferred to the small post office on the Island while Norman worked his way up the ladder to delivery. It was then they started to raise a family. Amanda Felton came along almost fifteen years ago and four years later, after multiple tries at having more children, Susan was diagnosed with a rare and incurable form of lung and rib cancer. She fought the good fight, but died when Amanda was just seven.

For the past seven years, Norman raised his daughter alone and from the enclosed photographs of her had done an excellent job of it. I studied several of the eight-by-eleven photos Jane included in the file.

Amanda was a beautiful, dark-haired, blue-eyed girl about five foot four inches tall and had the budding shape of a young woman. She was a B+ student and would be a straight A student if not for difficulty in her math classes. She played guard on the girls' basketball team and was a member of the cheerleading squad for the boys' basketball team. According to reports from Eaton and Hollis, she was a popular girl with many friends on the Island and mainland.

There was a list of friends interviewed concerning Amanda's disappearance. She was last seen at school on Friday as normal. She rode the ferry home after school with several classmates who also lived on the island. They went their separate ways when the ferry docked and Amanda hadn't been seen since.

What were the odds that the disappearance of Amanda Felton and her father's beating the Montero kid were unrelated?

A billion to one.

"How long has school been back in session?" I said.

"Not long. A week when the incident took place."

"Amanda Felton had become Norman Felton's entire life," I said, thinking aloud.

Jane nodded. "Daddy's little girl," she said.

Still thinking aloud, I said, "Are the tapes from the cruisers available?"

"Yes, but they show nothing."

"Can I see them anyway?"

"Sure."

"The 911 call; was it the only one or did someone else also see the attack and make a call?" I said.

"Nothing else from dispatch," Jane said. "I'll check and get back to you."

"The response time, how long?"

"Under three minutes," Jane said. "You want exact?"

"As close to," I said.

"You're wondering if there was someone else on the field that ran off before my deputies arrived," Jane said. "Another witness."

"Just a detail."

"And a damn good one."

"When can I see the tapes from the cruisers?" I said.

"As soon as I can have them sent up," Jane said. "Tomorrow."

"I'll stop by on the way back from seeing Felton."

"What are you going to do now?"

"Go home and think," I said. "Mind if I keep that notepad?"

"This one is going to get messy, isn't it?" Jane said.

"I've never seen a neat one," I said.

To the right of my trailer, a few years ago, I'd set up a pull-up station, a push-up station, and a hundred and twenty-pound heavy bag on a tripod. Hanging from a nail on the side of the trailer were several weighted jump ropes.

Regan was still out with Oz when I returned home, so I changed into sweats and did a workout to clear my head and open the thought valve.

I started with some jump rope using a two-pound weighted leather rope. After ten minutes I worked up a sweat and put the rope back on the nail. Then I did some push-ups, elevated and flat, switched over to pull-ups and chin-ups, and then grabbed the bag gloves and gave the bag a pounding.

Norman Felton went berserk at the high school and beat the Montero kid with a baseball bat. Why?

When confronted by Jane's deputies Felton was still in such a rage he turned the bat on them. Why?

Felton's daughter, Amanda, was missing, but for how long was the question. Before or after he went Mickey Mantle on the Montero kid?

Somebody hurt Felton's little girl.

That's the only thing I could see that would set him off like that.

I thought about what I would do to somebody if they hurt mine.

Yeah, somebody hurt his little girl and on the surface it appeared that somebody was a skinny teenager from another country named Ubaldo Montero.

"Dad, don't you ever get sick of beating yourself up like that?" Regan said. I hadn't heard the car arrive over the loud creaking of the heavy bag hinges.

I lowered my hands and pulled off the gloves.

Regan held up her learner's permit. "Did you know Oz's brother runs the motor vehicle place?" she said.

"Actually I did, and let me guess and say Oz called in a few favors," I said.

"Only one," Oz said as he came up behind Regan. "He allowed her to take the written test today instead of all the usual BS. She only got one wrong and the kid never even read the book."

"I have to go to Rhode Island tomorrow," I said to Regan. "Want to go for a ride with your old man?"

"Can Mark go with us?" Regan said. "He's going nuts and needs to get away from Clayton for a day."

"Sure," I said. "Give him a call and ask, and I was thinking the three of us might go to dinner in town tonight." I looked at Oz. "If you change that shirt."

"You bought this thing," Oz said. "But for a free meal I'll dip into my wardrobe."

SEVEN

Walking between Regan and Mark, I guided them into the used cars section of Felton Motors. The franchise was one of the largest dealerships I've ever seen. The new car section stretched on for acres and while the used or pre-owned was only a third that, it was still vast and stocked with hundreds of late-model cars and trucks.

"In about a minute a shark disguised as a salesman or woman is going to descend on you like blood-soaked bait in the water," I said.

"You're not staying with me?" Regan said in a panic-stricken voice.

"I'll stay with you," Mark said.

"Like you know anything about buying a car," Regan said.

"As much as you do," Mark said.

"Relax, honey," I said. "Tell whoever comes out that you're just window shopping, but that you're interested in a one- or two-year old sedan with low mileage and still under warranty if possible. No foreign cars because repairs are too expensive once the warranty expires, and no color red. Too expensive to insure. Six cylinder with AC so you don't have to drive around drenched in sweat. Oh, automatic transmission, no stick. Any questions?"

"What if . . . what if I find something I like?" Regan said.

"I'll talk to the salesman after my meeting," I said. "We can put a hold on it for up to a month without losing our deposit."

Regan nodded.

"You're on your own," I said and walked toward the front office.

"What should we get?" I heard Mark say behind me. "Something fast."

"We?" Regan said.

The showroom was modern with six desks occupied by six salespeople, three males and three females. There was also a reception desk manned by a plump woman with an honest to God beehive hairdo.

"John Bekker for Mr. Felton," I said. "He's expecting me."

Beehive glanced at her computer screen. "Yes, he is."

Robert Felton's office was twice the size of a regular living room. The desk was cornered, modern and large with two computers atop it. At least a hundred framed photographs adorned the three walls facing the desk. A round oak table with four chairs sat on top of an Oriental rug centered in the room.

Robert Felton stood up and walked out from behind his desk. He was a tall man, as tall as me, with a strong chin, blue eyes and thinning, brownish hair. The light blue suit he wore didn't come off a rack and the Italian shoes on his feet cost more than my entire wardrobe.

"Bob Felton," Felton said and extended his right hand.

We shook. His handshake was a bit too firm in the way some men feel they have to prove their grip to you so you know they are the alpha male in the room.

"Coffee or a soft drink?" Felton said.

"Coffee's fine," I said.

"Let's sit at the table," Felton said. "It's more comfortable."

We took chairs opposite each other and no sooner had we touched down than the office door opened and Beehive came in with a silver tray that held a matching coffee pot, creamer and two cups.

Beehive set the tray between us and looked at Felton. "Hold your calls?" she said.

"Please," Felton said.

Felton waited for Beehive to leave before he reached for the silver pot and filled both cups. He added cream to his, looked at me, waited for me to nod and then added cream to mine.

We both sipped. The coffee was excellent.

"I've already spoken by phone to your sheriff and told her everything that I know," Felton said.

"I know," I said as I dipped into my suit jacket for a mini tape recorder. "But sometimes when you go over stuff a few times something new develops."

"Are you recording this?"

"It helps me later when I play it back," I said. "Sometimes I'll remember a question I forgot to ask or realize something I missed the first time. Okay."

Felton nodded.

"So tell me about your brother, his life, daughter, whatever pops into your mind," I said as I hit record.

"Norman is a good man and a good guy," Felton said. "He loved his wife and Amanda with everything he's got. He even loved working for the stupid post office. I started this franchise ten years ago and tried to get him to partner with me, but he wanted to get his pension first. After his wife died, I worried about him a lot, but he pulled things together and he and Amanda seemed very happy together on that island."

"How often did you see him?" I said.

"Let's see now," Felton said. "Thanksgiving, Christmas, sometimes New Year's. Memorial Day, the 4th, Labor Day, Amanda's birthday and maybe one or two more times a year."

"Eight, maybe nine times a year?" I said.

"Sounds about right."

"Tell me about his personality," I said.

"Personality?"

"Was he warm, cold, violent, like that?"

"Oh," Felton said. "Well, as a kid he was pretty much normal. Good grades, played some sports and was the usual pain in the ass kid brother. As a man he was a straight shooter all the way. The kind of man who wouldn't pad an expense report even if he could get away with it because it was wrong. He taught that to Amanda as well."

"Did he have a temper?" I said.

"God, no," Felton said.

"How can you be so sure? Losing a wife can change a man."

"It did," Felton said. "It brought him and Amanda even closer."

I took a sip of coffee. "Do you have any idea why he took a baseball bat to that Montero kid?"

"No, do you?"

"Did you know he owned a baseball bat?"

"No, I didn't," Felton said. "They had a bunch of basketballs and a hoop in the backyard. Amanda played for her school team."

"What about Amanda?" I said. "What kind of a kid is she?"

"The best kind," Felton said. "Respectful, decent grades, good at sports, did most of the cooking the past few years. Made the turkey dinner all by herself last Thanksgiving. I got a drawer full of Christmas, birthday and Father's Day cards from her since she learned how to write."

"What about enemies? Did your brother have any?"

"Enemies? Like what, dogs? He delivered the fucking mail, for God's sake."

"That doesn't mean there isn't someone who has a grudge against him."

"No, it doesn't," Felton said.

"Mr. Felton, after a week the police and FBI databank has produced not one lead into Amanda's disappearance."

"By police you mean that Mickey Mouse sheriff's department they got handling this?" Felton said.

"Sheriff Morgan is a highly experienced and very efficient law enforcement official," I said. "I've known her twenty years and worked with her many times."

"She's so fucking great, why'd she hire you then?"

"I have an advantage," I said. "I'm not bound by the county limits."

Felton looked at me for a moment and then slowly nodded.

"Back to Amanda, do you know if your brother was having any problems with her?" I said.

"Like what?"

"Like any normal headaches fourteen-year-old girls give their fathers, especially when Mom is no longer around."

Felton thought for a moment, then sighed softly. "I honestly can't say," he admitted. "As I said, I only saw them eight or nine times a year and whenever Norm and I spoke on the phone he never brought up any problems they might have been having at school or at home."

"When did you last see them?"

"Fourth of July a few months ago," Felton said. "I went there for a few days."

"And?"

"And everything was normal."

"Did you bring your wife and kids on the visits?" I said.

"Used to," Felton said. "Before the divorce seven years ago. Now I go alone."

"Mr. Felton, do you have any experience with the law?"

"You mean have I ever been arrested?" Felton said. "No."

"I didn't necessarily mean that," I said. "The way an

investigation works is through facts and evidence. The 'play a hunch' and 'sixth sense' bullshit is for movies and cop shows. The facts and the evidence guide the investigation in a direction and that direction only changes when new facts and evidence dictate it."

"In English that means?"

"Your brother took a baseball bat to a kid at a high school his daughter doesn't attend, for reasons unknown, on the same day Amanda apparently disappeared," I said. "Since both your brother and the kid are unavailable to talk to and Amanda is missing, there are no known reasons for the attack and disappearance at this point. Unless your brother or the kid wakes up and starts talking or a ransom note for Amanda shows up in the mail, every little detail no matter how small is important. So what I need you to do is think long and hard and try to remember anything your brother might have said that could potentially be a problem with Amanda, and while you're at it, about Norman himself. No matter how small, no matter how insignificant. Work it out in your mind and then call me on my cell phone." I removed a business card from my wallet and slid it across the table.

Felton looked at the card and then picked it up and tucked it into his shirt pocket. "Mr. Bekker, my brother could die or that kid could die and my brother goes to prison for a very long time. I need you to find Amanda and bring her back safe. I'll raise her as my own and on that I give you my word."

"I'll do whatever I can to make that happen," I said.

Felton nodded.

"My kid is out there picking out a car so I'll be back in a week," I said. "That should give you enough time to think over what I asked and make some notes."

"Your kid is picking out a car? Here?" Felton said.

61

"Come out and say hello," I said. "This should be good."

Regan chose a two-year-old Impala with thirty-six thousand miles on it and under warranty for another twenty-four months. She asked the salesman to hold it for her for one week and Felton approved the request. The car was silver with four doors and all the options of a new car.

"I don't get it," Mark said. "There are plenty of places to buy a car back home."

"True," I said. "But just because Regan gets her license doesn't make her an experienced driver. Only driving does. Next week I'll have Oz come down with us and he'll drive my car home while Regan drives her Impala."

"Me?" Regan said.

"Her?" Mark said.

"And Mark and I will be passengers."

"We will?" Mark said.

"Yes."

"On one condition."

"What's that?" I said.

"We go shopping?"

"For?"

"A suit of armor," Mark said and eyed Regan.

I sat with Oz at the new patio table and played the tape I'd made of the session with Robert Felton.

Regan and Mark were down at the beach tossing a Nerf football. Molly slept on the new table directly to my left and I rubbed her ears lightly.

"Man sound on the level to me," Oz said.

"I think so," I said. "Tomorrow get out your pen and notebook and write down our conversation."

"All of it?"

"Yup."

"I'm paid by the hour, right?"

"Don't milk it," I said. "Or I won't let you drive my car next week."

"Why I want to drive your rusting heap next week, or any week for that matter?"

I told him.

"Little girl growing up," Oz said.

"And her father's growing old."

"Join the club," Oz said. "You get your AARP application in the mail yet?"

"Hell, I've been throwing them away for years," I said.

Eight

Detective Philip Eaton was around Jane's age, a hard-looking man in a well worn suit with dark eyes and thinning brownish hair. Detective Stan Hollis, a bit older, had the look of a no-nonsense cop highlighted by a crew cut that made him look like Jack Webb in the movie *The DI*.

Along with Jane, we met in her conference room. She ordered a pot of coffee from the deli across the street. I brought a dozen donuts from Pat's and we happily sipped and munched our way through the meeting.

Eaton and Hollis had dozens of photos of Midnight Island, including aerial shots of a twelve-acre pond in the woods, which encompassed forty percent of the Island.

"We used our K-9 dogs to search the Island for Amanda Felton, and two teams from the State Police," Hollis said. "Every square inch with no results."

"The IFW Game Wardens sent two divers to cover the pond and found nothing," Eaton said. "It's only fifteen feet deep at the center and anything on the bottom would have been found."

"Sewers and drainage systems?" I said.

"Checked and rechecked, even by the dogs," Hollis said.

"The Felton home?" I said.

"Searched top to bottom," Eaton said. "By us, a couple of State Police investigators and the dogs. If something's missing, we can't find it."

"Any signs of forced entry?" I said.

"None, but the garage door was open and the front door unlocked," Hollis said.

"We think whatever set Felton off caused him to leave in one hell of a hurry and he forgot to lock the door and close the garage," Eaton said.

I grabbed a lemon cream donut and took a bite. I looked at Jane and she happily sunk her teeth into a chocolate éclair. I washed my bite down with a sip of coffee and said, "What about athletic equipment? Did you find any in the house and garage?"

"Basketballs," Hollis said. "There's a hoop in the backyard. One of those with a water filled base. Nothing else."

"You checked around to see if Felton purchased a baseball bat?" I said.

"He didn't," Eaton said. "At least not in this state."

"Did he own any weapons?" I said.

"If by weapons you mean guns or knives, no," Hollis said. "The kitchen has one of those knife racks for cooking and there's several could cut an arm off, but none are missing."

"How are his finances?" I said.

"Owes another four years on the mortgage and has never missed a payment," Eaton said. "Has a nice nest egg in his federal pension and a few investments made through a planner at his bank. We found three thousand in his checkbook and twenty-five thousand in a savings account for Amanda's college. No major purchases, no outstanding credit card balances, no loans and an insurance policy for one hundred thousand payable to Amanda. He was a good provider and responsible parent."

"Any money in the house?" I said.

Eaton grinned. "He's old fashioned in that regard. We found one of those accordion folders in the desk in the living room. You know, with the sections that stretch out. He marked the sections Grocery, Emergency, Amanda Allowance, Entertainment and Miscellaneous. There was two hundred dollars in grocery, a hundred in Amanda, two hundred in entertainment, five hundred in emergency and two fifty in miscellaneous."

"And three hundred and nine dollars in small bills in a piggy bank on Amanda's bureau in her room," Hollis said.

"Her allowance money?" I said.

"Has to be," Hollis said.

"What about friends and neighbors?" I said. "I know you interviewed dozens, anything stand out?"

"Pretty much across the board it's agreed Felton is a good neighbor, friend, citizen, concerned parent and so on," Hollis said.

"No reports of trouble from a neighbor of any kind," Ellis added.

I nodded, sipped from my cup and thought a moment. "Did he have a home computer?"

"No," Ellis said.

"Cell phone?"

"We ran the numbers in his cell phone," Ellis said. "Mostly work, a few calls to his brother, some friends on the island, nothing connected."

"Hard line?" I said.

"Same," Ellis said. "Amanda has an extension in her room. Calls mostly to her dad at work, her friends, things like that. Nothing out of the ordinary we saw."

"What about the bat?" I said. "How many sets of prints were on it?"

"Who can say," Eaton said. "Prints were smeared with blood and there wasn't one useful print that would hold up in court. The blood and hair on the bat came from the Montero kid."

"What about the bat itself?" I said. "Is it new or used?"

"Used?" Hollis said.

Jane looked her question at me and shifted her weight in her chair.

"A brand new bat off the rack is unmarked," I said. "Once you start batting some balls around it takes on markings and in some cases, if hit hard enough, the seams of the ball are imprinted on the wood. If used in a game there might even be some pine tar on it."

Hollis and Eaton looked at me.

"Bekker played minor league ball," Jane said. "He was good enough to get drafted by some big league teams. Phil, why don't you go to evidence and get the bat."

"While he does that, let's take five," I said.

Jane and I stood on the steps of the Public Safety Building directly in front of the *No Smoking Sign* where she lit a cigarette and I smoked the electronic one.

"How long a ride to Midnight Island?" I said.

"From here, about a half hour."

I glanced at my watch. It was just after ten. "If you aren't tied up I'd like to take a ride out there and check the house," I said. "I'll spring for lunch."

"Need the boys to go with us?" Jane said.

"Ask them what their schedules look like," I said.

Jane nodded.

We puffed on our cigarettes.

"Are you going to stick with that thing?" Jane said.

I tucked the electronic cigarette into my pocket. "I'd rather face the Wrath of Khan than the wrath of my daughter."

I wore latex gloves while I examined the baseball bat. It was a 32-ounce off the rack from any sporting goods store, a million-a-year-produced model made from maple. I rotated the barrel and carefully inspected every square inch of it.

The dried blood appeared black and covered much of the barrel and handle, but I could see markings where the bat had struck ball, including the clear markings of baseball seams burned into the wood.

I showed the markings to Jane and the two detectives.

"I can't say for sure it's a game bat or just for practice, but it's seen a few balls," I said.

Hollis took the bat and gave it a once-over.

"When you spoke with the Montero kid's foster parents and the high school, was he active in sports at all?" I said.

"School says no, foster parents said the boy was big into soccer," Eaton said. "But then so is everyone south of Texas."

I nodded. "How is the 800 hotline doing?"

"A few calls early on that led nowhere," Hollis said. "Nothing since."

I looked at Jane. "Can we see the video shot from the patrol cars and then I'll wrap this up?"

The DVD shot from the camera in Deputy Spears's cruiser filmed the left side of the field with the high school in the background. I studied the image for signs of shadows and movement, something to indicate there was somebody else on the field, but I saw nothing.

The angle from the Andrews cruiser showed more of the right side of the field, but was also devoid of anything I could call useful. After watching both several times, I was about to ask Jane to turn the DVD player off, when I felt that tug in my brain and said, "Show me Spears again."

We watched it again.

"What?" Jane said.

"One more time," I said.

We watched it again.

"I don't know," I said. "Can you burn me off a copy of each?"

"No problem," Jane said.

"Let's go, then."

"I'll be on the Island," Jane told the detectives. "Want to join us?"

"I have court at two this afternoon," Hollis said.

"I'm free," Eaton said.

"Good," Jane said. "Bekker has promised us lunch."

NINE

The Felton home was about a mile from the ferry point on Midnight Island. Jane drove her cruiser and I asked her to stop in the drop-off zone for a moment. I got out and stood by the railing where the ferry had docked a few minutes earlier. Besides the cruiser there was just one other car getting off.

Jane and Eaton joined me. I sucked on my electronic cigarette while Jane smoked a real one. I looked at the ferry, the open ocean in front of us, turned and read the posted sign for a bus schedule.

A bus circumvented the island one hour before the scheduled ferry ride to the mainland. A special bus picked up kids returning from school at four and four-thirty.

"The Felton home is about a mile from here?" I said.

"I clocked it," Eaton said.

"Did she normally ride the bus home or walk?" I said.

"The drivers said they sometimes remember her and sometimes not," Eaton said. "We think she would walk on nice days and ride in bad weather."

"Did she walk home the day before the incident?" I said.

"The drivers can't say," Eaton said.

"What about her schoolmates who rode with her on the ferry?" I said. "Any of them remember walking home with her or sitting with her on the bus?"

"The ferry yes, walking home or the bus no," Eaton said.

"The drive to the Felton home, is it the same as if walked?" I said.

"Straight run down this road with a left turn for two blocks," Eaton said.

"Is there a shortcut, maybe through some wooded area?" I said.

"Not that I know of," Eaton said. "But it doesn't seem likely. Most of the woodlands with the pond are past the Felton home to the east."

"Jane and I are going to walk," I said. "We'll meet you there."

Eaton nodded. "Remember where it is?" he said to Jane.

"It will be the house with the patrol car in the driveway," Jane said.

Eaton got behind the wheel of Jane's cruiser and drove out of the drop-off area and onto the street. Jane and I followed and stepped onto the sidewalk.

I paused to look around. The center of town wasn't much. A small diner, a hotel/restaurant combination where I had lunch with Carol many years ago, a few shops and stores, a large grocery store, a tiny post office where Susan Felton must have worked, gas station, and that was about it. And at the very end of the drop-off area, a satellite ATM machine from a large bank on the mainland.

I walked closer to the ATM, followed by Jane.

"Jane, did they . . . ?" I started to say.

"No, they did not," Jane said with anger in her voice.

We looked at the circular hole in the top right-hand corner of the ATM machine where a live camera was aimed at the general height of the person using it. The camera had a range of at least one block and would have picked up anybody walking past it in either direction.

Including Amanda Felton on the Friday prior to the Saturday she disappeared.

"How long do they keep recordings?" I said, as I jotted down the bank phone number for customer use.

"I'll call them from the Felton house," Jane said.

We crossed the street and slowly walked past the center of town and along the tree-lined street toward the Felton home. Once past the center there wasn't much to see. Homes, front lawns, gardens, a small senior center and rest home, more lawns and gardens, more homes.

"A pleasant walk," I said.

"An easy place for a snatch and grab," Jane said. "I haven't seen one person on the street since we left the ferry."

We covered the mile in about twenty-five minutes or at about a snail's pace. If I expected to find something or have a revelation about Amanda's disappearance, one wasn't forthcoming.

Eaton was standing beside Jane's cruiser in the fifteen-foot-long driveway of the Felton home. "A few neighbors poked their noses out to see what's going on, but I shooed them inside," he said.

I stopped and looked at the driveway, garage and front of the home. It was a modest but well kept Tudor, white with green trim, a large patch of lawn left of the driveway, now overgrown, and a tall wood fence that shielded the backyard.

"Where do you want to start?" Jane said as she fished a key from her shirt pocket.

"Backyard and basement," I said.

Jane opened the unlocked gate and we entered the backyard. As backyards go, it was fairly large with an overgrown lawn on the left side and a cement area on the right. The water-based basketball hoop rested on the fringe of the cement. The kitchen door was a glass slider. A small patio table with two chairs and a barbeque grill took up most of the patio space.

"Forensics find anything meaningful back here?" I said.

"The county boys and the state police lab went over every

square inch and got nothing," Eaton said.

"Basement accessible from inside?"

"The key only works on the front door," Jane said. "Wait here."

She scooted around to the front of the house and a minute later she slid the kitchen door open from the inside.

"Basement door is off the kitchen," Eaton said.

I opened the door and we walked down the steps and entered the basement. A long time ago, probably before his wife died, Felton had started to finish the basement. Two of the cement walls were paneled in walnut. Apparently the project ended with his wife's death.

I know the feeling.

Besides the oil burner and air-conditioning unit, there was a workbench with some tools, a lawn mower, a few rakes and that was about it.

"Losing his wife knocked the steam out of him," I said. "Whatever plans he had for making the basement a family room ended when she died."

Jane looked at me and nodded.

The living room was well furnished and comfortable with sofa, chairs and table that went back to the time the home was purchased. Felton hadn't updated since his wedding, including the non-digital television that wouldn't have worked without cable. The room was devoid of family photographs.

Felton's bedroom was basic, with a queen-size bed, expensive dresser with mirror, a full bathroom and walk-in closet. The closet held his clothes and shoes. Except for a dozen photographs of his wife on the dresser and nightstand beside the bed, there was nothing to say a woman once occupied the bedroom.

Same for the bathroom.

The medicine chest held toothpaste, razor and blades, shaving cream, aftershave, a bottle of aspirin, and IB. The shower shelf held shampoo and a bar of soap. On the sink was a brush and comb, a toothbrush in a stand, a bottle of mouthwash.

His wife's entire array of junk and feminine stuff had long ago been removed.

Amanda's room, smaller than her father's, was bright and cheery with a colorful bedspread, drapes, dresser, a full-size bed, peach carpet, a small desk for schoolwork. Her closet held all the clothes a fourteen-year-old girl wears, with a healthy supply of shoes and sneakers.

On the dresser a small jewelry box held earrings, necklaces, bracelets, watches, and her mother's engagement and wedding rings. The piggybank that held her allowance money was a large ceramic pig.

"She keep a diary?" I said.

"None that we found," Eaton said.

I looked at Jane. "Did you keep a diary at fourteen?"

"All girls do," Jane said.

"We didn't find one and the entire house was searched by three teams at least twice," Eaton said. "Even the dogs didn't sniff one out."

I looked at the ceramic pig. "What was the amount she has?"

"Three hundred and nine dollars in mostly five-, ten- and one-dollar bills," Eaton said. "No loose change."

"The bottom open up?" I said.

Eaton nodded. "Latex gloves were worn when the money was counted."

"Anything look missing from this room?" I said.

"Hard to say when you don't know the exact contents," Eaton said.

"I agree, but if you were fourteen and decided to run away from home, would you leave three hundred and nine dollars sitting on your dresser?" I said. "And your jewelry and clothes?" I walked over to the desk. "Dusted?"

"Yes," Eaton said. "We found just the girl's prints that match what was lifted off her stuff in the bathroom."

I pointed to a closed door. "In there?"

Eaton nodded.

A thick red binder was open to the section for math. She'd started her homework the Friday night before my wedding. Several problems were solved. Several were not. I flipped through the binder. There were sections for English, Geography, History, Science, Composition, Social Studies, World Events and Miscellaneous.

"How much was in the Amanda's Allowance folder in Felton's desk?" I said.

"A hundred in tens," Eaton said.

"Ten a week, you figure," I said. "Thirty-one weeks missing a buck in her bank."

"Sounds right," Eaton said.

"No, it doesn't," Jane said. "When I was fourteen I spent my allowance as fast as I got it. That piggy bank is for something else, from somewhere else."

I flipped through the section marked Miscellaneous. She'd written different categories in it: *Birthdays of family and friends. Holiday cards to buy. Family phone numbers and addresses. Books to read. Movies to see. School events. Jobs. The Barrett family. The Stewart family. The Wright family. The Crawford Family. The Butler family.*

"Jane, what do you think this is?" I said.

Jane looked over my shoulder, as did Eaton.

"She babysits," Jane said.

"That's where the $309 came from," Eaton said.

"Recognize any of the names from your interviews?" I said.

"No, but we interviewed neighbors on the same block," Eaton said. "These families could live on the other end of the Island and maybe even on the mainland."

"Find out," Jane said. "As soon as we get back."

Eaton pulled out a notepad and pen.

"Just take the binder," Jane said.

Eaton closed the binder and tucked it under his left arm. "Anything else?" he said.

"Yeah, let's go to the backyard again," I said.

We went downstairs to the kitchen, where Jane opened the sliding doors and we stepped outside. As soon as Jane slid the door closed I shoved her against the fence.

"Hey, what . . . ?" Jane said.

I shoved her again. Behind me I could hear Eaton drop the binder.

"Pull something and you'll eat your teeth," I told him.

"What's wrong with you?" Jane said.

"We've been friends twenty years, so when you ask me for a favor I expect you to be honest with me," I said.

"What are you . . . ?" Jane said and I shoved her again.

"That's enough or I'll cuff you," Eaton said.

"Don't even think about that, you idiot," Jane said to Eaton. "And quit shoving me before I kick you in the balls," she warned me.

"Goddammit, Jane," I said, turned and took a chair at the patio table. I pulled out my electronic cigarette and sucked on it.

Jane came to the table and took the second chair. As she sat, she pulled out her pack and lit a cigarette.

"When you asked me to get involved in this case you said you needed my special skills," I said. "Two men who lost their wives and had to raise a young daughter alone. Two lonely men who cracked up because they couldn't deal with the pain. You want me to get inside his head because I've been there and done that."

Jane inhaled on the cigarette, flared her nostrils and exhaled smoke.

"Maybe because I can relate to him I can see something others can't," I said. "Get in his head and see what makes him tick."

"It's possible," Jane said.

"And if I get too close and . . . fall off the wagon, are you going to hold my hand?" I said.

"That's not going to happen, Bekker," Jane said. "You know why? Because you hate to repeat yourself."

"What the fuck's going on here?" Eaton said.

"Shut up," Jane said. She inhaled, blew smoke, looked at me. "At the risk of kissing your ass, you're the best goddamn cop I've ever known. Better than Walt and he's pretty fucking good. So maybe I thought a little what you said, so what? There's a father shot, a kid with his brains bashed in and a young teenage girl missing and I need your help. Like Eastwood said, a girl's got to know her limitations."

"I don't think Eastwood quite put it that way," I said. "Let's go to lunch."

"You buying?" Jane said.

"You two are fucking nuts, ya know that?" Eaton said.

The Midnight Island Hotel restaurant served a mean burger and fries, and I called Paul Lawrence at his FBI office in Washington while we ate.

"I was just thinking about you," Lawrence said.

"Me or the donuts I ship you for a favor?" I said.

"That constitutes a bribe," Lawrence said.

"Three dozen okay?"

"Bribe away."

"There's a girl lost in the system," I said. "Been missing about a week. Her father beat up a kid at the high school and a deputy accidently shot him. He and the kid are both in a coma. The missing girl is his daughter. I'm working with the sheriff's department on this one. Maybe she's at a hospital out of state somewhere or got picked up by Social Services, you never know."

"Unless you look. Give me the particulars and I'll do some checking," Lawrence said.

I gave Lawrence names, dates, the events, what I had and didn't have and guessed about.

"A week missing isn't a lot of time," Lawrence said. "Generally the system works slower than that, but I'll see what I can do."

"Thanks."

"How's the family, Janet?"

"Regan is fine," I said. "Learning how to drive. Janet is in Chicago for work and not all that pleased with me at the moment."

"Women never are," Lawrence said. "Don't forget the . . ."

"Donuts, yeah I know," I said.

I hung up and set the phone aside.

Jane looked at me. "She'll come around," she said. "You're a prize and women hate to give up their prizes."

"Even if the prize came from a box of Crackerjack?" I said.

On the ferry ride back to the mainland, Jane and I stood at the front railing and smoked cigarettes. The salt sea air that rose up from the ocean waves was a fine mist on our faces.

"This mist is ruining my hair," Jane said. "It's all frizzy."

"Feel like tagging along while I talk to the families Amanda babysat for?" I said.

"When?"

"Tomorrow around seven or so in the evening," I said. "They should all be home by then."

"It's the least I can do since you've made more progress in one afternoon than we have in a month," Jane said.

"And since you threatened to kick me in the balls," I said.

"You were shoving me."

"You lied to me."

"I didn't lie. I just left a few things out."

"That's kind of like leaving a few things off your tax returns, isn't it?"

"Oh, shut up."

Jane slid her left arm around my waist and I placed my right arm around her shoulder.

"That miserable prick I'm married to goes nuts when my hair is frizzed," Jane said. "When I get home he'll take two of those goddamn blue pills."

"You know what they say," I said. "You can't keep a good man down."

Jane allowed herself a tiny laugh. "Asshole," she said.

TEN

Regan tossed a log into the bonfire I'd built in the trashcan I kept in front of the trailer for just such a purpose. Red embers rose up and blew away on the soft breeze off the ocean.

She sat in the chair next to me at the new table, lifted her cup of tea and took a small sip.

"Say I get my license and we buy that car," she said. "How are we paying for it? I could crack open that trust fund Eddie Crist left me."

"Not necessary," I said. "Besides, that's your what-if-and-when money."

"What if and when what?"

"What if something happens to me and when I'm no longer around," I said. "Crist wanted to guarantee you'd be taken care of under those circumstances."

"Dad, don't talk like that," Regan said. "I've had enough of homes, special schools and helmets to last forever."

"I know, but you're a young lady now and life has surprises and you have to be ready for them," I said.

Regan sipped some tea.

I had my usual mug of coffee and sipped some of that.

We set our mugs down on the table.

"I still don't get what happened between you and Aunt Janet," Regan said. "When she explained to me about Chicago she sounded so . . . cold. I never heard her like that before."

"She's upset with me and rightfully so," I said.

"Because you stayed in Hawaii?"

"I think because she wanted to come to Hawaii and show her support and understanding, and I told her no," I said. "And in telling her no I pushed her away. Pushing someone away is the same as shutting them out and nobody likes to be shut out of someone's life that they love."

"So you were wrong?"

"In a sense," I said. "But what I tried to explain to Janet and failed miserably is that I needed time to work out what just happened. It wasn't as if I lost a job or a close relative or had to put my dog down. A woman who I went there to confront died because I confronted her. I just needed the extra time to come to grips with that."

"So Aunt Janet was wrong?" Regan said.

"I don't think either of us is wrong," I said.

"That doesn't make sense."

"A lot about relationships doesn't make sense," I said. "So it's late and I need to do some work."

"Is that why the TV is outside?"

"Yes."

"You won't stay up too late?"

"No."

Regan stood up and kissed me on the cheek. "Night, Dad."

"Where's Molly?"

"Are you kidding? She's already under the covers."

"Go join her."

After Regan went inside I removed the DVD discs Jane gave me and inserted one into the player on top of the TV.

After thirty minutes of alternating DVDs, I was about to give up for the night when I spotted something in the background of the Spears recording.

I hit pause and leaned forward.

A speck or spot in the background against the high school.

I wiped the screen and it stayed put. Maybe the speck was a spot on the camera lens in the patrol car. I went inside the trailer, dug around the cramped kitchen drawers and found the old magnifying glass I kept for just such situations.

I returned to the television and held the magnifying glass to the spot. The round speck could have been anything, anything at all, but it was bugging me and I needed to know why.

I called Jane on her cell phone. It was late, but she wasn't asleep.

"Bad news about the tapes from the ATM machine," Jane said. "Information gets dumped after one week if a hold isn't requested on it. My guys and me fucked up on that one."

"I doubt except for Felton driving onto the ferry it would have provided us with much anyway," I said.

"Amanda could have been in the car with him or a passenger on the ferry without him knowing," Jane said. "We screwed up, Bekker. You can say it."

I didn't.

"How good is the county forensics lab?" I said.

"Not good enough," Jane said. "What do you need?"

"Can they enlarge and augment frozen images off the DVD from the patrol cars?"

"C'mon, Bekker, do you know what the county budget is?" Jane said. "Something like that we'd ship to the state lab. Want me to call them?"

"Hold off on that for now," I said. "I'll ask Walt if they can do it."

"What have you got, anyway?"

"A speck."

"Of?"

"That's what I want to find out," I said. "Check Spears's

camera in his car, see if a speck or smudge shows up on the lens."

"That I can do," Jane said.

"I'll call you tomorrow."

"We still going to interview those families?"

"Six o'clock ferry okay?"

"Meet me at my office," Jane said. "Five-thirty."

I hung up and called Walt.

"Thank God you called," Walt said. "I worked late and was about to sit down to one of Elizabeth's pot roast dinners."

"It can't be that bad," I said.

"Burned roast and raw potatoes cooked in the same pan," Walt said. "How she does it is beyond me."

"Take the woman out for dinner and do yourself a favor," I said.

"Speaking of favors," Walt said.

"I need one."

"Really?" Walt said sarcastically.

"I have a DVD taken from the camera of Deputy Spears, one of Jane's, and I need an image blown up," I said. "Can you do it?"

"I can't. I can barely tie my shoes," Walt said. "But Venus can."

"Around noon?" I said.

"Gonna cost ya."

"I know."

"Gotta go," Walt said. "Elizabeth's serving this evening's heartburn."

I hung up and set the phone on the card table. The fire in the trashcan crackled lightly, begging for another log, but I held off and let it burn out. I sucked on the electronic cigarette for a bit and mulled things over.

Then I packed away the DVDs and went inside to grab some sleep.

Eleven

Regan was locked into her driving with laser-like focus as she steered my Marquis through rush hour traffic toward the highway.

Oz had to keep a commitment with his brother and promised to take her out later. I had some time to kill and decided to see what my little girl had learned.

If she was nervous at all she did a good job of hiding it.

"On the test, merging into highway traffic is a biggie," I said.

Regan nodded.

"You have to merge smoothly into traffic and then change lanes without endangering traffic," I said.

Regan nodded again.

"And the instructor is going to look for turn signals, use of mirrors and speed limits," I said.

Another head nod.

"And the instructor may ask questions he or she expects answers to besides a head nod," I said.

"Sorry, Dad," Regan said. "I'm concentrating on driving."

"I know," I said. "But realistically you may be listening to the radio, have coffee in the holder, a passenger talking, kids in the back, a barking dog, snow or rain and the wipers on, and you're expected to drive safely and not be distracted. Your instructor knows that. So should you."

"You're saying I should relax more?" Regan said.

"If you grip the wheel any harder you're gonna break it off,"

I said. "Look at your knuckles. They're white."

Regan grinned and relaxed a bit.

"Entrance coming up on the right," I said.

Regan clicked on the blinker for a right lane merge and eased the car into the lane. A hundred yards down the road she braked and took the near-hairpin turn onto the entrance ramp. Traffic was light and she guided the Marquis into it, accelerating with the left blinker on until she had fully merged.

When she reached the speed of sixty-five, Regan clicked on the left turn signal and merged into the center lane.

She grinned.

"Dad, when you were a cop did they teach you special driving?" she said.

"If you mean high-speed chases and such, yes."

"Can you show me?"

"Don't you think you should pass your test first?"

"I don't mean teach me, show me," Regan said. "I have very little memories from when you were a cop."

"Do you know how to get to the trailer from here?" I said.

"Sort of. Maybe. I don't think so," Regan said. "Don't you?"

"Oh, you'll make a good lawyer," I said. "Next exit coming up, get off."

In the parking lot adjacent to the beach, we switched places.

"Lock in," I said as I adjusted the mirrors and seat.

Regan snapped into her seatbelt as I put the Marquis into first gear and drove slowly onto the hard sand of the beach.

In low gear, the engine was so slowed that twenty-five miles an hour put it into the red zone. I floored the gas and switched into drive, and the sudden release of the gears jolted the Marquis to sixty miles an hour in a matter of seconds.

I raced along the sand for a hundred yards or so, then feathered the brake and turned the wheel to the left. As the car turned, I braked hard and brought us into a three hundred and sixty-degree spin.

As we came out of the spin, I centered the wheel and hit the brakes, bringing the car to a quick and jolting stop. Immediately, I flipped the car into reverse and floored the gas until we reached thirty miles per hour, feathered the brake and turned the wheel right, braked and brought us into a reverse spin.

As we came out of the spin, I hit the brakes and screeched the Marquis to a stop close to the marking of the first stop.

"There's another way to quick start the acceleration, but I don't think it would work on sand," I said.

"No problem."

I looked at Regan. Her face was pale.

"My father is an amusement park ride," she said.

I grinned. "Want to drive us to see your Uncle Walt?"

"Can I practice that spinning thing?"

"No."

Regan held the door for me as we entered the police station because my arms were full with three dozen of Pat's Donuts finest.

We walked to the desk sergeant behind the long counter. "Here to see Walt," I said. "He's expecting me."

The desk sergeant eyed the boxes in my arms. I set one on the counter.

"For the boys," I said.

"I'll tell the Captain you're on the way up," the desk sergeant said.

Before Regan and I reached the stairs, the desk sergeant had the box open and was happily biting into a lemon cream.

At the top of the stairs we walked past the detectives' division, the lieutenant's office, and stopped in front of Walt's walnut-colored door. Regan knocked and said, "Uncle Walt?"

"I'm too sick and too tired to get up," Walt said from behind the door.

Regan grinned as she opened the door and we entered.

"What's the matter?" I said.

"My wife's pot roast," Walt said. "What did you think?" Seated behind his desk, Walt eyed the two boxes in my arms. "Regan, your daddy is a very evil man."

I set the boxes on the desk. "One for the detectives, one for Venus," I said.

Walt looked at the top box. "I only have six detectives," he said, opened the box and removed a Boston cream.

"I thought you said you were sick," I said.

"This is better than Tums," Walt said as he tore into the donut.

"Can I have one?" Regan said.

"Let's all have one," I said.

Regan grabbed a chocolate with sprinkles and I opted for the lemon frosted.

"Who's the third box for?" Regan asked.

"It's payment for Venus," I said.

"Who's Venus?"

"A very busy police officer who has a lot better things to do than putz around with your dad's special requests," Walt said.

"And you pay her in donuts?" Regan said.

"She has four hungry kids at home," I said.

"Can I meet her?"

I nodded to Walt.

Walt shoved the last bit of donut into his mouth and stood up. "Let's get this over with," he said.

On the way out of Walt's office, I dropped the box of nine off at the detectives' squad room where it was immediately pounced upon like sharks on bloody prey.

Venus had a special office behind the desk sergeant's counter. Venus is Venus Jackson-Brown, a beautiful black woman in her mid-forties that took my mind to a young Pam Greer. She had two desks and three computers where she performed daily analysis for the department.

From behind the desk against the window, Venus looked at us, focused on Regan and showed us her dazzling smile. "Would you look at this child," she said as she stood up.

"My daughter, Regan," I said.

"Hi, Regan," Venus said. "And aren't you grateful."

"For what?" Regan said.

"That you don't look like your daddy," Venus said.

Regan looked at me and cracked up laughing.

"It isn't that funny," I said.

"Yeah it is," Walt said.

Venus eyed the box. "Is that for me or are you playing out the cop stereotype?"

"It's a bribe to get you to do my dad's bidding," Regan said.

Venus laughed and said, "This child has got you pegged, Bekker."

"And wrapped around her little finger," Walt said.

"I promise to only use my power for good," Regan said.

I set the box on the desk and pulled the disc from my jacket pocket. "If we're done picking on the old man here, I need something enlarged on this disc," I said.

Venus looked at me, and then shifted her eyes to Regan.

"She can stay," I said. "She wants to be a prosecutor one day so she might as well get used to the boring and mundane now."

"Let's see what you got," Venus said and took the disc.

She slid the disc into a DVD player tray and we watched the monitor as the screen lightened and the field and high school background came into view.

"And what do we need?" Venus said.

"Wait a second," I said. "There. Pause it."

Venus hit a button and the image froze.

"See that speck there in the lower left hand corner," I said and pointed. "Can you enlarge and augment that?"

"On my computer," Venus said.

She switched out the DVD player for one of her computers and ran the disc. We gathered around the monitor while she clicked her mouse and tapped some keys. Slowly, the image shifted and centered on the speck. With the mouse, Venus enlarged the speck and increased the definition until it was almost identifiable.

"Can you go more?" I said.

"I can double it," Venus said. "Any more than that and resolution is lost."

"Go ahead," I said.

Venus used the mouse to enlarge the image, and as it grew, the image became clear and identifiable.

"It's a busted window," Walt said.

"Yeah," I said.

"I don't get it," Regan said.

"Me, neither," Venus said.

The window, first floor or basement, had a circular hole with a spiderweb pattern around it, the kind made when something is thrown through it.

Something like a baseball.

"Can you print a few copies of that?" I said.

"Gonna hang them up on telephone poles?" Venus said as she clicked print.

"Or somebody's back," I said.

Venus removed several copies from the printer and handed them to me. "Drop in again, Bekker," she said. "The next time you're in the mood to supply the Brown family with some delicious treats."

★ ★ ★ ★ ★

As Regan and I walked to the Marquis, she said, "Can I drive us home?"

I flipped the keys to her. "Might as well, seeing as how you have me wrapped around your little finger."

Regan caught the keys and grinned at me. "Like I said, I'll only use my power for good," she said and unlocked the car door.

TWELVE

Jane and I stayed in her cruiser as we rode the ferry to Midnight Island for the second time in two days. I dug out the electronic cigarette and then removed the folded printout from my shirt packet and gave her that, too.

"What's this," Jane said as she lit a real cigarette.

"The speck on the Spears recording," I said.

"That's a busted window," Jane said.

"It is."

"At the high school."

"It is."

"Off the cruiser camera?"

"It is."

Jane looked at me.

"About the right size of a baseball when hit through a reinforced plate glass, wouldn't you say?" I said.

Jane looked at the printout. She inhaled and blew smoke out through flared nostrils. "I would."

"So maybe the Montero kid wasn't alone that day," I said. "Maybe he and another kid were hitting fly balls around the field and maybe one of those fly balls went through the window. And maybe the other kid took off when Felton showed up out for blood and maybe that's where . . ."

"Felton got the bat," Jane said. "From Montero."

"Yeah," I said.

"That's a lot of what ifs."

92

"Yeah."

Jane looked at me again as she inhaled on the cigarette. She exhaled smoke through her nose and her face hardened. "This would mean we have a possible witness."

"Yeah."

"Is that all you have to say is 'yeah'?" Jane said.

"Boat's docking," I said.

Armed with the addresses, we decided to go nearest to furthest and make a loop back to the ferry to catch it back to the mainland before the last run.

The Barrett family was up first. Jonas Barrett, his wife Amy, and their two sons, Jonas Jr. and Peter, occupied a two-story brick home a half mile down the same road as the Felton home.

Jonas was an architect. Amy was an accountant. Both had small offices in their basement so they could work from home several times a week. Amy answered the door when Jane knocked. A pretty woman close to forty, she was momentarily taken aback at seeing Jane in full sheriff's garb.

"Yes?" Amy said.

"Mrs. Barrett, I'm Sheriff Jane Morgan and this is my associate John Bekker," Jane said. "We'd like to talk to you about Amanda Felton. May we come in for a few moments?"

"I'm making dinner, but yes, come in," Amy said.

Amy and Jonas sat on the sofa while Jane took a La-Z-Boy chair and I opted to stand behind Jane.

"That poor family," Amy said. "Such a lovely girl and very responsible for only fourteen."

"Mrs. Barrett, how often did Amanda babysit for you and when was the last time she watched your boys?"

Amy looked at Jonas. "I'm not sure," Amy said. "Two, maybe three months ago. We don't go out often."

"The awards dinner," Jonas said. "My company has an annual dinner for best design and things like that. We just made the last ferry back. She sat for us that night from six to midnight."

"Not since?" Jane said.

"No," Jonas said. "We're kind of homebodies."

"Our boys are five and six and they're a handful," Amy added.

"What did you pay her?" I said.

"Five an hour," Jonas said. "Is that important?"

It was when you considered the piggybank money that sat on Amanda's dresser.

"No," I said. "Just curious."

"Is there anything else?" Amy said. "I have to see to dinner."

The Wright family lived just three blocks from the Barretts in a two-story modern home with a nice front lawn and a large backyard that showcased an above-ground swimming pool.

The Wrights were an older couple without young children at home. They did have two small poodles, however, and those small poodles were spoiled beyond comprehension. So spoiled that they required a sitter whenever the Wrights went out for the evening or the poufy pair would wreak havoc and destruction upon furniture, rugs, beds and anything else they could get their little pink paws into.

Amanda Felton was a wonderful girl and so good with the babies, Mrs. Wright told us. It was a shame what happened to her and they hoped we would be able to find her.

At ten dollars an hour she was worth every penny and they would never get a professional to sit at that price.

Rebecca Butler, recently divorced, had custody of her five-year-old daughter and used Amanda regularly on weekends because dating was hard enough, but almost impossible when you have a five-year-old at home. "The decent ones are scared away when they find out you have a kid," Rebecca explained.

"When did Amanda sit for you last?" I said.

"Two weeks before she disappeared," Rebecca said. "She was supposed to sit for me that Saturday. I had to cancel my date and he was a good one."

Driving to the next house, Jane said, "No surprise that woman is divorced."

"Who's next?" I said.

"Toss-up between the Crawfords and the Stewarts," Jane said. "Their houses are on the same block at the end of the island."

About a mile down the road, the homes became sparser and the road narrower as the island came to a point. On the final block before the road made a hairpin turn back toward the ferry there were just five houses.

The Stewart home was second in, so we stopped there first. The Stewarts were a young couple with a six-year-old son who was crazy about Amanda, so they said.

"We only get out once a month or so and when we found Amanda we felt really lucky to have her," Mrs. Stewart said. "We're really upset by what's happened. I hope you find her soon."

"Did Mr. Felton deliver and pick her up?" I said.

"Oh, yes, and they were always very prompt," Mrs. Stewart said. "It's really a shame what's happened."

"Yes, it is," I agreed.

The Crawford home was a large, two-story Tudor with a lush front lawn and huge backyard protected by a tall picket fence.

Michael Crawford was a widower seven years. He was around forty-five years old, a tall, well-put-together man with thinning brown hair and a small goatee. He had a pot of coffee going and invited us to join him for a cup at the kitchen table.

"My wife died when my daughter was just one," Crawford

said. "My son, James, is eighteen now and off to college next year on a scholarship. He's captain of the high-school football team and the best quarterback this state's ever had. He also plays basketball and some baseball, but he's a football man all the way."

"Mr. Crawford, how often and when did Amanda last sit for you?" Jane said.

"Every Sunday during football season," Crawford said. "My daughter isn't a fan. Norman would drop her off around ten in the morning and she would stay until we get back around six or six-thirty. She would have sat for us the Sunday before she . . . went missing."

Jane and I turned around when the front door opened and James Crawford came rushing in. Dressed in a tank top and running shorts, he was dripping with sweat.

"Dad, is everything okay?" James said in a panic.

The kid was enormous. I put him at six foot four, two hundred and twenty-five pounds and all of it muscle.

"Relax, James, they're just asking questions about Amanda Felton," Crawford said.

"Doing roadwork?" I said to James.

James nodded. "Six miles a day except weekends during the season. I add an extra day during the off-season."

"The high school is going to win the state championship this year hands down," Crawford said. "And after that the colleges will have a dogfight over James. Right, son?"

James nodded. "I need a drink."

Crawford nodded as James turned and went into the kitchen.

"Since Amanda's . . . since her disappearance we've dropped my daughter, Steff, off at my sister's on the mainland before the games on Sunday," Crawford said.

"Mind if I get a glass of water?" I said.

"Help yourself," Crawford said. "There's bottled in the fridge."

I walked into the kitchen where James was standing in front of the open refrigerator, guzzling green Gatorade from a bottle. He lowered the bottle and looked at me.

"I could use a cold glass of water," I said.

James grabbed a bottle of water from the refrigerator and handed it to me. "The tap water sucks," he said as he closed the door.

I removed the cap from the plastic bottle and took a sip. "I was a baseball man myself," I said. "Never played football."

"What position?" James said.

"Pitcher, but I could also hit a bit," I said. "Got as far as Double A ball."

"I quit the baseball team as a junior," James said. "I'm a better quarterback than center fielder and Dad thinks it's my ticket to college and the pros."

"Is it?" I said.

"If we win the state game I'll have forty scouts at the front door with scholarship offers," James said. "Full one hundred-percent Monty."

"You mean full scholarship?"

"Complete."

I sipped and nodded. "So what can you tell me about Amanda?"

James took a swig from the Gatorade bottle. "Good kid," he said. "I didn't really see her much, but my kid sister Steff liked her a lot and she always seemed happy to babysit her."

"Did you know Mr. Felton?" I said.

"Only from dropping her off and picking her up," James said. "Seemed like a good guy."

"What's the gossip at school?" I said.

"Wow," James said. "Like everybody was shocked at what

97

happened. I didn't know the Montero kid much, but he seemed like a decent guy who tried to fit in and . . . what's the word I'm thinking about?"

"Assimilate?" I said.

"Yeah."

"Did he play baseball?"

"Not that I know. Why? Oh, the bat."

I nodded. "It strikes me as odd that a kid from a soccer country would be at the high school on a Saturday with a baseball bat by himself."

James shrugged his massive shoulders. "Maybe he wanted to learn how to play?"

"Alone?"

"I don't know," James said. "I think he might have been a volunteer for the school's groundskeepers. They touch up the field on Saturday before a game. Maybe that's why he was there?"

"Most likely," I said. "Well, thanks for the water."

"Sure."

I walked to the kitchen door and paused to do a Columbo and look back at James. He was sipping from the Gatorade bottle.

"By the way, what was lacking in your game at center field?" I said.

James shrugged his giant shoulders again. "Poor depth perception," he said. "I couldn't judge a fly ball. They tried moving me to the infield, same thing. A pop up became a nightmare. It's weird because I can judge distance when throwing the ball, just not when it's coming at me."

"Sounds like a mild form of astigmatism," I said.

James nodded. "Yeah. No big deal. It doesn't bother my game at quarterback."

"I wish I could tell you more, but all I can say is I hope to

God you find the girl alive," Crawford was telling Jane when I returned to the living room.

"Thank you for the time, Mr. Crawford," Jane said.

I held up the bottle. "And the water."

"What do you think, Bekker?" Jane said as she drove her cruiser along the road back to the ferry.

"I think we learned Amanda is a responsible girl," I said. "She had two jobs lined up for the weekend she disappeared and that poses the chicken or the egg question: Did she disappear because her father went nuts, or did her father go nuts because she disappeared? Want to check out the high school tomorrow, say around noon?"

"Broken window?" Jane said.

"Broken window."

"I'll be there."

THIRTEEN

I sat with Oz for company at the new table and rehashed the interviews from earlier, looking for and failing to connect the dots.

Maybe the dots just weren't there.

Maybe they were connected in places I hadn't looked yet.

I was mulling things over when my cell phone started ringing off the hook.

"Bekker, Jane," Jane said. "Bad news."

"What?"

"Norman Felton died about twenty minutes ago."

"How?"

"Heart attack," Jane said. "The hospital called me and said they did everything possible, but his body was worn out from the gunshot wound and a blood clot developed on the heart."

"This just got a whole lot more difficult," I said.

"I got to do a quickie news conference at the hospital," Jane said. "Maybe the added publicity will shake something from the tree?"

"Maybe," I said. "What about the Montero kid?"

"I'll check on his status," Jane said. "Want me to call you back?"

"I'll be up for a while."

Oz went in while I talked to Jane. He returned with a pot of fresh coffee and filled our empty mugs.

I set the phone down and puffed on the electronic cigarette

while I thought.

"You think the girl is dead?" Oz said.

"What I think doesn't matter," I said. "The evidence is what matters. If this was a kidnapping for ransom case and ransom wasn't paid within seventy-two hours, the girl would probably be dead. If this were a sexual predator case the girl would definitely be dead. If she ran away from home on her own accord, she's probably alive and in hiding somewhere, scared and alone."

"So what's the evidence tell you?" Oz said.

"That Norman Felton beat Ubaldo Montero within an inch of his life and that Amanda Felton is missing," I said.

"Not a lot to go on," Oz said.

"No."

"Maybe this Montero kid's not as innocent as you think?" Oz said.

"Who said I thought he was innocent of anything?" I said. "But that isn't the question."

"No?"

"The question is innocent of what?"

Oz looked at me.

I inhaled on the electronic cigarette and blew a soft ring of vapor smoke.

My phone rang again. I checked the incoming number. It was Paul Lawrence in Washington.

"I was hoping you'd still be up," Lawrence said.

"I'm having too much fun to sleep," I said. "What's up?"

"I put the Felton girl into the system," Lawrence said. "Nothing yet, but I have some ideas of my own. I'll let you know if anything pans out."

"Thanks, Paul."

"You got anything?"

"The girl's father just died," I said. "Heart attack from a

blood clot."

"Sorry to hear that," Lawrence said.

"Call me when you have something," I said.

I set the phone aside, picked up my mug and took a few sips. The phone rang again. I checked the number and answered the call. "John Bekker."

"Mr. Bekker, Robert Felton," Felton said in a weak voice that told me he'd been crying. "I just got off the phone with the hospital."

"I heard and I'm sorry," I said.

"My brother didn't deserve to go out this way," Felton said.

"No," I said.

"My niece?"

"I'm working the evidence," I said. "I won't lie to you, it's a difficult one."

"What about the FBI? Shouldn't they . . ."

"I already have them involved," I said. "A close friend is an agent in Washington. He's running a file."

"Bekker, I'm all that girl has now," Felton said. "Find her."

"I'll see you in a few days, Mr. Felton," I said. I set the phone aside again and placed the electronic cigarette beside it.

"Maybe you should turn the damn thing off for tonight?" Oz said.

"I told Jane I would wait for her call back," I said.

"Mind if I turn in then?" Oz said.

"Go ahead," I said. "I'm not good company right now anyway."

Oz nodded, stood and walked down the beach to his trailer.

Jane didn't call back for another hour. I sat and waited, drank coffee and puffed on the e-cigarette to kill the time.

"Bekker, the kid isn't responding well I'm afraid," Jane said when she finally called. "The doctors say his brain keeps swelling up and they have to go in and relieve the pressure. He's still in a coma."

"We're stuck at the starting gate for the moment," I said.

"Something else," Jane said. "Montero's father showed up at the hospital. His English isn't that good, but he got his point across."

"What did you tell him?" I said.

"That we're doing everything that we can, what did you think?"

"Did you ask him if his son ever expressed interest in playing baseball back home or learning how?"

There was a pause in the conversation.

"Goddammit, Bekker," Jane said.

"Fill me in tomorrow when we meet at the school," I said. "I'm going to bed."

"Lovely," Jane said and clicked off.

I went into the trailer, checked on Regan who was sleeping peacefully with Molly curled up at her stomach. The trailer was dark and quiet with just nightlights and a lamp on in the living room.

I filled a glass with milk and sat at the tiny kitchen table.

I'm not sure why but I suddenly wondered how Joey Fureal was doing. Had she left for Sloan yet and if she had, was she settled into the hospice near the hospital?

"Dad?" Regan said. "What are you doing?"

"Having a glass of milk. Thinking."

Regan filled her own glass from the container and took a seat. Immediately Molly jumped onto Regan's lap and meowed for some milk.

"Thinking about what?" Regan said after she sipped. "Aunt Janet?"

"This girl I met in Hawaii not much older than you," I said. "She has cancer of the bone marrow and is supposed to go to New York for treatment. I was just wondering how she is."

"Do you have a number to reach her?"

"Sloan-Kettering Hospital and a hospice."

"Call her and find out," Regan said. "I'm sure she would love a phone call."

"I think I will," I said. "Maybe tomorrow afternoon."

"Is she going to . . . ?"

"I don't think so," I said. "She's a lot like you. She's a fighter."

Regan stared at me for a moment.

"Sometimes it's really hard to fight, Dad," she said. "Ya know?"

"I do."

Molly went from lap to table and sniffed Regan's glass.

"Can I tell you something really bad?"

"Sure."

"I try real hard not to think about Mom," Regan said. "I know that may sound selfish or childish of me, but my last memory of her was . . ."

"You don't have to go there," I said.

"I know," Regan said. "But for years and years and years if I thought about Mom I would wake up screaming from nightmares. I would bang my head on the wall to make them stop and the only way they would stop would be if I never thought about Mom. Is that why you drank so much?"

"Yes."

"I'm learning to drive and taking some courses at college next semester and maybe I'll never be exactly what you would call normal, but I don't ever want to go back to that dark place," Regan said.

"I know."

"So maybe that girl could use a friend to talk to?"

I nodded. "I'll call her and see. Okay?"

"Okay."

"In the meantime Molly has her head stuck in your glass," I

said. Somehow Molly had pushed her face into the glass and was lapping up the milk.

Regan pulled Molly out. "Come on you little thief," she said. "Good night, Dad."

Regan carried Molly to her bedroom and turned off the light.

I finished my milk and thought about the Montero kid, Amanda Felton, baseball bats and broken windows, and tried to make some sense of it all.

I couldn't.

I thought about Janet. During the Koch investigation, Melissa Koch hired a pro out of Hawaii and put a hit on us. He caught me off guard while we were having a picnic at the beach and would have killed us if Janet hadn't fought back. She got beat up pretty badly and required some surgery and a facelift afterward, but the few seconds she gave me to recover allowed me to overcome and kill the bastard.

Maybe Janet interpreted my staying in Hawaii as selfish and uncaring about her?

Maybe that's how it appeared to her?

That wasn't the case.

I needed to explain that to her, to find the right words to tell her how much she meant to me and somehow convey to her that my extended stay in Hawaii was for her benefit and not mine.

I thought about how selfish that sounded.

I called it a night and went to grab some sleep.

FOURTEEN

I was thirty minutes early in meeting Jane at the high school, so I picked up a coffee at the deli across the street, sipped it, sucked on the electronic cigarette and kept a lookout for a cruiser.

I spotted Jane's cruiser at five minutes before noon, tossed the empty coffee container into a trash bin and crossed the street. She had just parked in the school visitors' lot when I walked up to her car.

"Waiting long?" Jane said as she got out.

"Not really," I said. "Let's go see the principal first."

"I bet you saw the principal a lot when you were a kid," Jane said.

Alan Dixon was in his eleventh year as principal of the high school, a point he made several times when Jane and I stopped by. He was a roundish, middle-aged man with glasses and mousey brown hair. He struck me as a go-along-to-get-along kind of guy.

Dixon came out from behind his desk after his secretary showed us into his office. "I don't know what else I can tell you that I haven't already on your first two visits," Dixon said to Jane.

"This is John Bekker, a special investigator retained by the county to help with this investigation," Jane said.

Dixon looked at me, but didn't offer to shake my hand.

"I see," he said. "And how can I be of help to you?"

"The teacher who made the 911 call, is she here?" I said.

"Mrs. Johnson, yes she is," Dixon said. "I'm not sure where at the moment, but she's in the building."

"Can you page her for us?"

Dixon looked at me.

"I wasn't asking," I said.

We met Sheryl Johnson in the teachers' lounge. Dixon insisted on being present and even though Jane could have refused him she allowed him to stay out of courtesy for his position. The teachers' lounge was near capacity as the next two periods were dedicated to lunch breaks.

Sheryl Johnson, a tall, stately woman in her mid- to late forties, came off as one of those dedicated teachers who wouldn't retire until she was forced to or died in the classroom. It wasn't an act; she was the real thing.

"My next class is in forty-five minutes," Sheryl said.

"We'll be quick," I said.

Sheryl nodded politely.

"I listened to your 911 call several times," I said. "You told the operator that you were on the third floor."

"That's correct," Sheryl said.

"And in your statement to the detectives you said you were working that Saturday to prepare for the teacher/parent meeting the following Monday," I said.

"Also correct. The first one of the new year."

"You told the dispatcher you were on the third floor and could see Mr. Felton beating Ubaldo Montero with a bat," I said.

"Correct, except that I didn't know who they were at the time."

"Did you see or hear anything before the incident started?" I said. "Yelling, an argument, loud voices or noises?"

"No, I did not," Sheryl said. "As I told the detective and put in my statement, I was in another room away from the windows and didn't hear or see a thing until I entered the room from where I called 911."

"What time did you arrive at the school on that Saturday?" I said.

"As I told the detectives and put in my statement, I arrived—" Sheryl said.

"She's been over this countless times," Dixon interrupted. "I don't see—"

I spun around and looked at Dixon. "Nobody said you could talk."

"You can't speak to me that—" Dixon said.

"Jane, throw him out."

Jane stood up.

"All right, I'll be quiet," Dixon said.

I looked at Sheryl. I could see amusement in her eyes. "Go on."

"I arrived at the school around eleven-thirty that morning," Sheryl said.

"And you called 911 around two-thirty in the afternoon," I said.

"Yes."

"And from eleven-thirty until the time you called 911, you heard nothing and saw nothing unusual?" I said.

"If you mean on the field, I spent most of the time in the library and teachers' conference room," Sheryl said. "And the windows in those rooms don't face the athletic field."

"When you arrived at the school that Saturday, was there anybody on the field?" I said.

Jane looked at me.

Sheryl looked at me. "Funny, but the detectives didn't ask me that."

Dixon looked at Sheryl, nodded and then looked at me.

"Was there?" I said.

"The volunteer field crew that takes care of the field," Sheryl said. "I should have brought that up myself, but since no one asked I didn't think it was important."

"How many in the crew?" I said.

"I didn't count them," Sheryl said. "I walked past the field to the main entrance. I would guess maybe six."

"Was Montero one of the six?" I said.

Sheryl closed her eyes. I could see the gears working in her mind as she thought back and tried to picture the field on that Saturday.

I looked at Jane. Her lips were a tight, hard line and her eyes were slits.

Suddenly, Sheryl's eyes snapped open. "Yes!" she said excitedly.

"Working on the field?" I said.

"Yes."

"Did you recognize the others?" I said.

"I think one of them might have been Carl Noth. He's in my first-period class."

I looked at Dixon.

"I'll get him," he said.

After Dixon left the room, I chatted a bit more with Sheryl. The information well had run dry after the Noth kid, but you never know where a question or innocent remark might lead.

Carl Noth was a tall kid, skinny as a rail, blond, blue-eyed and a senior. He appeared a bit nervous when Dixon escorted him in and asked him to take a seat.

"Am I in trouble?" Noth immediately asked.

"Should you be?" I said.

"I haven't done anything," Noth said and started biting his lower lip.

"Then why did you ask?" I said.

Noth shrugged his bony shoulders.

"Do you know Ubaldo Montero?" I said.

"Sure. We have a few classes together and we both volunteer for groundskeeper work for extra credit," Noth said.

"That Saturday he was beaten up you worked on the field," I said.

Noth nodded. "We usually get there around ten and work a few hours on the grass and lines, the end zone, stuff like that."

"That day, what time did you finish up?"

"Maybe one or so, a bit earlier."

"Did you all leave together?"

"We put all the equipment away in the field shed and then left," Noth said. "I got my own car and gave two of the guys a ride. I don't know about the others."

"Could he have stayed behind?"

Noth shrugged again. "Could have. I don't know. Why don't you ask him?"

"Because he's still in a coma," I said.

Noth lowered his eyes. "Sorry."

"The equipment shed, do you have a key?" I said.

"No," Noth said. "There's always a custodian on Saturday. He lets us in and locks it when we leave."

"The others in the group," I said. "Write down their names for me in case I need to talk to them."

Dixon escorted Jane and me to the custodial office in the basement. Its windows faced the football field. The custodial superintendent, Mathew Watson, met us in his cramped but neat office.

Dixon walked us in and said, "Sheriff Jane Morgan and her

associate John Bekker. They need a few moments with you."
Then Dixon walked out.

"Pull up chairs," Watson said. "They're not fancy, but they
are comfortable. I got a pot of coffee going on the burner if
you're interested."

"We'll each take one," Jane said.

Watson filled three ceramic mugs that had the school logo
imprinted on them and set two on the desk.

"Were you working that Saturday when Ubaldo Montero was
attacked by Norman Felton?" I said.

"Right to the point," Watson said. "Yeah, I worked that day.
Came in at five in the morning and left around one in the
afternoon right after I locked up the equipment shed."

"Any of them playing baseball, maybe hitting fly balls around
the field?" I said.

"No, but funny you should ask that," Watson said. "On
Monday there was a broken window in my office made by a
baseball."

"Which window?" I said.

Watson pointed to the center window opposite the desk.
"That one."

"Did you find a ball?"

Watson slid open a desk drawer and produced a well worn
baseball.

"Jane," I said.

Jane dug a plastic baggie from a pocket and held it out to
Watson. He dropped the ball into it.

"Who fixed the window?" I said.

"I did on Monday," Watson said.

"See anybody on the field on that Saturday besides the
volunteer group?" I said.

"No, but I wasn't looking," Watson said. "I have a four-man
crew on Saturday and there's a lot of work to do to get ready

for Monday."

"What's in the equipment sheds?" I said.

"What do you mean?"

"I mean what's stored in them?"

"Mowers, rakes, a couple of line spreaders, shovels, paint, weed whackers, stuff like that," Watson said.

"What about sporting equipment?" I said.

"That's kept inside the school in a storage facility under lock and key."

"Any chance this baseball came from there?"

"Who knows," Watson said. "Could be a game ball that got tossed during a game. It's football season now so not many are playing baseball."

"Someone was," I said.

Watson nodded. "I don't want to sound out of line here, but all this is leading up to what?"

"The early assumption is that Mr. Felton brought the baseball bat with him to the field," I said. "It may be that the Montero kid had the bat with him and Mr. Felton took it away from him."

"What difference does that make? He beat the kid half to death," Watson said.

"Intent," I said. "If Felton didn't have the bat with him when he showed up at the field his intent may have been just to talk to the Montero kid. If things got out of hand and Felton took the bat away from Montero, it changes things considerably. Montero could have been shagging fly balls with another kid and they broke your window."

"So what?" Watson said. "So they broke the . . ."

"The kid catching or hitting fly balls could be and probably is a witness," I said. "So here's what you're going to do, Mr. Watson. You're going to check your schedules and see who the four men you had working with you that Saturday are and you're going to have them report to the sheriff's department this afternoon where they will give statements to Jane and her detectives."

Watson looked at me.

"I wasn't asking," I said.

Walking back to Jane's cruiser, she was seething with rage. "When I get back to the office I'm going to de-ball my detectives and roast their useless nuts on my barbeque pit."

"Take it easy," I said. "They had a lot on their plate."

"They missed vital information, witnesses and who knows what else?" Jane said. "They'll be writing parking tickets on the beach when I'm done with them."

We reached the cruiser. Jane grabbed her pack and lit up a smoke.

"Goddamn amateurs," Jane said as she blew smoke through her nostrils. "There's a fucking witness, Bekker. A goddamn fucking witness." She was so mad, her cheeks were pink.

"And if we find the witness, that doesn't put us any closer to finding Amanda Felton unless the witness also happens to know where she is," I said. "Which I doubt. So save your blood pressure and take it easy on your detectives when you ream them out."

"Fuck my blood pressure," Jane said. "Where do you want to go, home?"

"That would be the place," I said.

I picked up Oz and Mark at Clayton's house and treated us to dinner at a family-style restaurant near the beach.

"Can we go to the trailer and make a bonfire?" Mark said.

"I don't see why not," I said.

"Maybe get some ice cream?"

"I don't see why not."

After dinner, while Regan and Mark tossed the Nerf football down at the beach, I loaded up the trashcan with firewood and built a roaring fire. Earlier, I'd picked up a half-gallon of chocolate ice cream. We sat around the fire and ate dishes of the treat and listened to the crackling of the wood.

"I never thought I'd say this, but I miss my mom," Mark said.

Seated to his left, Regan reached over, placed her arm around Mark and gave him a soft hug.

"Tell her that," Regan said.

"She left you the emergency number to reach her in Chicago, right?" I said. "Use my cell phone."

Regan nodded. "Call her."

I held my cell phone out to Mark. He took it, stood up and walked down to the beach to make the call.

"Maybe you should make a call of your own," Oz said to me.

FIFTEEN

"Thought you'd like to know I interviewed all four maintenance men who work for Watson myself," Jane said when I answered my cell phone.

Oz stepped out of my trailer with two mugs of coffee. He set them on the patio table and took a seat.

"And?" I said.

"The four of them pretty much say what Watson said," Jane said. "Saw the volunteer crew, they clocked out, went home and that's about it."

"The baseball?"

"Has more prints on it than Pat's has donuts. Most of them are useless, but we got one thumb print that belongs to the Montero kid, so there's no doubt he stayed late and was hitting or catching fly balls."

"Are you home?" I said, glancing at my watch. It was after eleven.

"Yes."

"Tomorrow, have the lab check the bat and ball for signs of seam imprints on the bat," I said. "I'll bet they find some that match the ball."

There were a few seconds of silence on the line, and then Jane said, "It's been almost two weeks, Bekker. If we find that girl, it won't be alive."

"Assuming she's been kidnapped, I agree with you," I said.

"You're angling she ran off on her own?" Jane said. "That's

my original feeling, but why hasn't she contacted anybody after the news of her father's death?"

"I don't know," I said. "Maybe she's in a place where she can't get local news?"

"Yeah."

"Maybe she's too scared to make contact?"

"Yeah."

"Let's make another trip to the Felton house tomorrow," I said.

"You miss something?" Jane said.

"I won't know that unless we see something new."

"What time?"

"Ten at the diner near your office," I said. "I'll spring for breakfast."

"What's going through that head of yours, Bekker?" Jane said as she dug into a western omelet.

"What did we learn from our previous trip to the Felton house?" I said.

"She babysits and kept a diary of her clients," Jane said.

"There's something else," I said. "I don't know what, but there's something else."

Jane ate some home fries, nodded and said, "There's always something else. Most times we never see that something else, or there would be no open and cold case files."

"I'm talking something close, something we missed," I said.

"You gonna eat your toast?" Jane said.

We arrived in the Felton driveway in Jane's cruiser around noon. Even in broad daylight I could see a light was on in the living room window.

"Did we . . . ?" I said.

"No," Jane snapped.

We opened the car doors in unison. As soon as we stepped out, the light in the window went dark.

"The back door!" I yelled.

Jane pulled her Glock as we ran toward the gate in the fence. Jane pushed on it. It was locked from the inside.

I stepped back and kicked the door in with my right foot, and caught sight of a boot going over the fence.

"Son of a bitch!" Jane shouted as we raced toward the fence.

I grabbed the top of the seven foot high fence, went up and over in one quick motion, and landed in soft grass. The sun was bright and I caught the movement of shadow in the nearby woods.

I took off running. Just as I reached the woods, I heard Jane come over the fence behind me.

"What, I'm a circus acrobat now!" Jane yelled.

I entered the woods and lost sight of the shadow, but I could hear the rustling of dry leaves and followed the sound. I ran about one hundred and fifty yards and stopped when I no longer heard the rustling noise.

Behind me I could hear Jane's footsteps on the dried leaves.

Options limited, I took off again in the general direction I last heard the rustling. I ran about a hundred yards and came to a well-worn hiking trail that forked in two directions.

I'd lost him.

I stopped.

Listened.

Behind me I could hear Jane running towards me. Dried leaves crackling, her heavy boots thumping.

Then, to my left flank behind me, I heard a second set of footsteps on dried leaves.

He'd doubled back.

I spun around and ran back in the direction I came. I ran about a hundred feet before a gunshot sounded directly ahead.

I stopped as the echo of the blast slowly faded and listened as one set of footsteps raced away from me.

"Jane!" I shouted as I took off again.

A hundred and fifty feet or so ahead of me, Jane was on all fours with her head down, right hand stretched toward her Glock, which was just out of arm's reach. I ran hard and reached her just as she collapsed onto her stomach.

"Jane!" I knelt beside her and rolled her over onto her back. She was semi-conscious with blood streaming down the left side of her forehead.

Beside the Glock was a thick tree branch the attacker had used as a club.

"Jane?" I said.

She opened her eyes and gave me a glazed-over look. I took her hands and gently lifted her to a seated position. "Can you stand?"

"I . . . think . . . so," Jane murmured.

I took her by the arms and slowly pulled her to her feet. She looked at me, gently rocked on wobbly knees and said, "Bekker, I don't feel so hot, ya know."

I caught her before she hit the ground, gathered up her Glock, then picked her up in my arms and walked back to the Felton home.

I was watching Eaton and Hollis dust the living room for prints when I heard Jane snarl, "Get the fuck off me, asshole."

I turned. An EMT from the ambulance I'd called was examining Jane's eyes with a flashlight. "I believe you have a slight concussion," he said. "I want you to go to the hospital for a complete check-up."

"How does it feel to want?" Jane said and sat up on the sofa. "Now get away from me before I taze your useless ass."

The EMT turned to his partner. "Let's go," he said.

"She sounds fine to me," Eaton said.

"Perfectly normal," Hollis added.

I walked to the sofa. "You really should get checked out," I said.

"I did," Jane said. "I think that son of a bitch grabbed a boob."

"I'm serious," I said. "Even a mild concussion can cause problems."

"Maybe later," Jane said. "I never saw the bastard until it was too late. He came out from behind a tree and all I saw was a tree branch in my face. I pulled my Glock and fired a shot into the ground, and after that I woke up here. What did you do, carry me back like Rhett Butler up the staircase?"

"And you weigh a bit more than the one-thirty-five you claim," I said.

Jane glared at me. "It's the boots and gun belt," she said.

"Jane, we got some new prints," Eaton said.

"Where?" Jane said.

"Window ledge."

"Must be when he spotted us," Jane said. "Dust the whole fucking house. Where he went will tell us what he was looking for."

"The whole house?" Hollis said.

"Every square inch," Jane said.

"I made some coffee," I said. "You want some?"

"No sugar," Jane said. "According to you I gotta watch my weight."

I entered the kitchen, filled two mugs with coffee and returned to the living room, where I gave Jane one and took a seat beside her.

"Gimme a smoke, will you?" Jane said. "Mine got squashed."

"And watch you pass out for the second time today?" I said. "Besides, all I have are those e-cigarettes."

Jane took a sip from her mug. "Who do you suppose that was and what was he after?"

"Evidence," I said.

"What evidence?" Jane said. "We tossed this place four times already. There isn't a goddamn thing here we can use."

"That we know of," I said. "Whoever was in here is scared and that means somebody knows more about Amanda Felton than we do."

"Like where she is and if she's alive?" Jane said.

"And what caused Felton to go berserk and what the Montero kid has to do with anything," I said.

Hollis came in from the hallway. "Jane, the closet where the vacuum cleaner was last time, it's not in there."

"Where is it?" Jane said.

"I don't know."

"He didn't break in here to steal a fucking vacuum cleaner and run through the woods with it," Jane said. "Find it."

I looked across the living room toward the closet where the Feltons kept their overcoats and jackets. The door was open just a crack.

"Got any gloves?" I said.

"What?" Hollis said.

"Closet door," I said.

I stood up and crossed the room. Hollis, gloves on, met me at the door. He grabbed the handle and opened it. The upright vacuum cleaner was stuffed among the jackets and coats.

Jane stood up and slowly walked to the closet.

"What the . . . I'm dizzy . . . fuck is going on?" Jane said. "A potential suspect drops in to do a little light housekeeping . . . I think I'm gonna puke."

She turned and sprinted down the hallway to the first-floor bathroom.

Eaton came in from the hallway and said, "What's going on?"

"Jane's puking and we found the missing vacuum," Hollis said.

"Dust it," I said.

I went to the front door, opened it and stood outside on the steps to puff on the e-cigarette. Anything at all can contaminate a crime scene. A hair off your head, a footprint with dirt across a rug, a spilled coffee. And that's what the house was now, a crime scene.

A few moments later, Jane joined me on the steps.

"My head's banging, Bekker," she said.

"I'm taking you to the hospital."

"I don't need . . ." Jane turned and vomited into the bushes that lined the front of the house.

"No arguments," I said.

Jane stood up. "I think I just puked up my spleen."

Hollis came up behind us. "Clean prints off the vacuum."

"Run them for comparisons," I said. "We might luck out and get a hit."

"Search every square inch," Jane said. "Twice. As soon as I get my second wind I'll join you."

"Go inside and sit," I said.

We returned to the sofa where we sat quietly for a few minutes while Hollis and Eaton combed through the house.

"Something was left behind he felt he needed to vacuum up," Jane said. "What?"

"Or found," I said. "Something so small it got caught in the rug piles."

"Like an earring backer?" Jane said.

"Or hair or nails or maybe a bit of dried blood?" I said.

"Except that I don't see any track marks in the rug," Jane said. "I don't think he had the chance to vacuum before we showed up."

"Yeah," I said.

We stared at the rug.

"Got any Luminol?" I said.

A few minutes later Hollis, Eaton and I stood in the living room with spray bottles of Luminol the detectives kept in the trunk of their car. Jane stood by the light switch with my cell phone camera at the ready.

Luminol is a chemical that, when sprayed on minute traces of blood, reacts with the iron content in the blood to glow a striking blue color. The room needs to be dim to see the blue and the effect lasts only about thirty seconds.

We sprayed about twelve square feet of white rug and Jane clicked off the light. After a few seconds of nothing, Jane turned the lights back on. We sprayed another twelve square feet or so and repeated the process when nothing glowed.

The fourth attempt, we struck pay dirt. Glowing blue in the dim light were speckles of blood residue centered in the living room. Jane snapped off several photographs before the effect faded, then turned on the lights.

"We need the lab," Hollis said.

"I'll call the state police," Jane said.

"Take too long," I said. "I'll call Walt."

While two crews of CIS investigators combed through the Felton house, Jane, Walt and I sat at the kitchen table and examined the photographs Jane took on my cell phone after feeding them into Jane's laptop computer.

"Somebody got popped," Walt said.

"Yeah, but when is the question?" I said. "And who popped who and why?"

"The day of the incident, what time did you gain access to the Felton home?" I asked Jane.

"By the time we got a judge to grant us access, around eight at night," Jane said.

"Enough time to do a quick cleanup on the blood and dry the rug with a hair dryer," Walt said.

"So why risk coming back to vacuum what you already cleaned?" I said. "Two weeks after the fact."

Hollis entered the kitchen with latex gloves on his hands. "Nothing inside the vacuum cleaner bag except dirt, hair and lint," he said.

"Make sure my guys get all contents," Walt said. "They'll analyze it at the lab."

"Want us to vacuum the whole rug?" Hollis said. "We might pick something up we can't see."

"Hold off on that for the moment," I said.

Hollis nodded and left the kitchen.

"Walt, how long will it take to get a metal detector over here?" I said.

"The lab boys probably got one in their car," Walt said.

It took only a few minutes before one of Walt's men got a hit with the metal detector as he scanned the living room rug. He knelt down and felt through the thick pile with a gloved finger and came up with an earring backer.

Jane took the backer, examined it and tucked it into her shirt pocket.

"Getting interesting," Walt said.

A few minutes later, about five feet from the spot where the backer was found, the detector hummed loudly again, indicating another find.

"Real interesting," Walt said.

Walt's man knelt down, dug around with his finger and said, "Got it."

The "it" was a diamond earring of about one karat.

Jane held it up to the light. "It's real," she said. "A gift from her father, probably."

I looked at the spot where the earring turned up. It was about five feet from the dried blood spatter.

"Want some coffee?" I said to Walt and Jane.

We took mugs out to the backyard patio table while Walt's men and Jane's detectives continued searching.

"Somebody popped the girl and the earring went flying a good five feet," I said. "It's a safe bet that somebody is who was in the house earlier and clocked Jane in the woods."

"How's your head, by the way?" Walt said.

"Like there's a tiny hunchback inside ringing a bell," Jane said.

"It's not a runaway case anymore," Walt said.

"No," I said.

"With Felton gone, that Montero kid in a coma and no witnesses stepping forward from the baseball bat incident, there's not a lot of suspects besides whoever broke in here to shed some light on things, is there?" Walt said.

"No," I said.

"A bat and a ball, a broken window, an earring that could have been lost a year ago and dried blood that could be left over from a kitchen accident is not a lot to go on," Walt said.

"No," I said.

"Is that all you're going to say is 'no'?" Walt said.

"He didn't break in here," I said. "When I carried Jane, the . . ."

"You carried her?" Walt said. "All the way from the woods?"

Jane glared at Walt. "What's that supposed to mean?" she said.

"The front door was unlocked," I said. "He had a key. His purpose was to find the earring or why else was the vacuum moved?"

"Why now?" Walt said. "Two weeks after the fact?"

"We touched a nerve," I said. "Somebody we talked to doesn't like us asking questions."

"How long is the list?" Walt said.

"Long."

"Jane, it's your case," Walt said. "Say the word and I'll loan you a pair of detectives, budget or no budget."

"Hold off on that, Walt," I said. "What we need is use of your lab and technicians at this point. Unless something breaks and we get a dozen suspects, we really have nothing new your detectives could work on."

Jane looked at me.

One of Walt's men poked his head through the sliding doors. "Nothing else, Captain," he said. "Want us to do room-to-room?"

Walt nodded. "And check for possible missing items."

"How do we do that when we don't know what was here to begin with?" Walt's man said.

"You figure it out," Walt said.

"Find some photographs of Amanda Felton and see if she's wearing those earrings," I said. "And check desks, tables, ledges for dust. There could have been an item there that's now missing. It would leave an imprint."

Walt's man nodded and ducked back into the kitchen.

"You don't miss much, do you Jack?" Walt said.

Jane inhaled on her cigarette, blew smoke out her nose and said, "We panicked somebody, Bekker. Somebody we talked to or maybe who's been watching the house. The son of a bitch could have killed me with that log he hit me with. The girl is probably dead by now, and the blood and missing earring are clues he didn't want us to find. Why is anybody's guess. We'd never have found them if he stayed away, so I'm thinking he thinks we know more than we do. Maybe we should let him think that for a while."

"Smokescreen?" Walt said. "That could work for a while, but

when nothing new emerges he'll feel pretty good we got zero plus nothing."

"A while might be all we need," I said. "Jane, can you call a press conference and make a statement that we now have a person of interest, but give no details?"

"Force his hand?" Jane said.

"He stuck his head up once, he might again if he thinks the pressure's on," I said.

"Turn up the pressure even more and announce that my department is now assisting you," Walt said.

"Highlight that eight-hundred number and up the reward for new info," I said. "Add that we now have additional clues."

Walt and Jane looked at me. "Like what?" Walt said.

I stood up and walked toward the gate. Walt and Jane followed me. I opened the gate and we walked to the front of the house where I led them to the spot where the intruder jumped the fence.

Between the fence and the street was a yard-wide layer of soft dirt where it looked like Felton was going to have fresh lawn put down. Beside my footprint and Jane's was a thick, deep print of a heavy boot.

"About a size thirteen I'd say," I said.

"Our man's a big fellow," Jane said.

"Walt, can your team make a plaster mold of this, maybe get a make on the boot model?" I said.

At the kitchen table, we looked at photos of Amanda Felton wearing the earrings in question. There was one photo of her fourteenth birthday where her father gave them to her as a gift. They were both smiling as Amanda held the earrings up to her ears.

One of Walt's men came in with a report. "We took a mold of the boot print, Captain," he said. "We'll do what we can to ID it at the lab. The blood on the rug is no good. A cleaning agent that probably had ammonia in it was used to remove the stains. A close examination of the rug fibers indicates a hair dryer was used as suggested to dry the rug before the suspect left. We got the bag from the vacuum just in case. Anything else?"

"What about missing items?" Walt said.

"Can't say. If we had a pre-incident inventory I could tell you."

Walt nodded.

"Anything else?"

"Do me a favor," I said. "Cover the outside of this house with as much yellow crime scene tape as possible. Really lay it on thick."

"No problem." Walt's man left the kitchen.

"Jane, park a cruiser in the driveway and leave it there," I said. "Have a camera on the dashboard recording the street with audio."

"I can do that," Jane said.

"On the way to the hospital, call that bank and tell them we want them to save the recording from that ATM machine for today," I said. "Maybe our big fellow came over on the ferry."

Walt looked at me. "Want a job, Jack?" he said. "I can ask to have you reinstated. Long hours for shitty pay."

"So who's going to the hospital?" Jane said.

Sixteen

"The hell I'm staying overnight," Jane snarled at the doctor in the hospital emergency room.

"A concussion, even a minor one can be serious," the doctor said. "Frankly, I'm a bit surprised you waited so long to get here."

"Crime doesn't stop because you get a bump on the noggin," Jane said.

"Maybe crime doesn't stop, but people do," the doctor said. "Now please get in the room and put on the hospital gown."

"You're joking," Jane said.

"I assure you I'm not," the doctor said.

"I have work to do," Jane said.

"Me, too," the doctor said.

Jane looked at me. "Bekker?"

"I never argue with doctors or women," I said.

"You're no help," Jane said. She looked at the doctor. "Give me the fucking gown."

At my trailer, steaks sizzled on the new grill while Walt and I watched the tapes from the ATM machine on Midnight Island.

Traffic was nonexistent from the mainland to the island until the four o'clock afternoon ferry.

Jane was clubbed around twelve-thirty in the afternoon. The first ferry back to the mainland after Jane's attack was at two and there wasn't one car on it, or the next one at three, or the one after that at four. Two cars rode the five and one rode the six and then nothing up until the final run except for us. Of the two cars on the five and one on the six, it was impossible to see clearly who was in them and the angle provided only partial plate numbers on the tags.

"Unless your man holed up for a few hours and was in one of those three cars going back to the mainland, he's either an island resident or found a secure place to hide," Walt said.

I got up to test the baked potatoes next to the steaks and flipped the steaks while I was at it.

"He could be staying at the Island Hotel or at one of the B and B's," I said as I retook my chair.

"Possible," Walt said.

"A big fellow with a size-thirteen shoe is going to drive a big car or SUV," I said. "He's not going to ride around cramped."

"I wouldn't," Walt said.

"So we're looking for a large man with big feet who drives a large car, who has a key to the Felton home and motive enough to break in and look for an earring," I said.

"When you put it that way it's open and shut," Walt said. "How's those steaks?"

"Almost done."

"Another way of putting that is slam dunk," Walt said.

I fished around for a fresh electronic cigarette.

"And yet another way of putting that is, there are about fifty thousand big guys with big feet who drive big cars in our county alone," Walt said.

I inhaled and blew vapor smoke. "The island has what, nine hundred or so permanent residents," I said. "Three thousand at the peak of summer. Half are women. Most of the men won't wear a size-thirteen shoe."

Walt did some quick math in his head. "Still talking five hundred or more men as possible suspects," he said. "Who has the manpower to conduct those kinds of interviews?"

"Eliminate the part-timers who weren't there two weeks ago when Amanda Felton disappeared and the number shrinks," I said.

"It do, don't it?" Walt said.

I got up and removed steaks and potatoes from the grill, and we ate watching the sun touch down on the horizon.

If it weren't for the fact we were discussing the probable murder of a young girl we could have been just two old pals enjoying a steak and the sunset.

If.

That word again.

But for the death of Amanda's father, Mr. Felton might have told us what this was all about.

But.

If Ubaldo Montero would just wake the hell up he could maybe shed some much-needed light on things and provide a much-needed break in the investigation.

If.

That damn word again.

When I was a kid of seven or eight and used the words *but* or *if* as an excuse not to do my chores or why I failed a test in school, my mother would say, "If *ifs* and *buts* were candy and nuts we'd all have a Merry Christmas."

"I could have the three cars returning to the mainland run down to see who owns them," Walt said. "I could also check the hotel and B and Bs' guest lists. Something might pop."

"Maybe," I said.

"But you don't think so."

"No."

"Well, what do you think?"

"I don't think I'm going to find Amanda Felton alive," I said. "I think this has gone from missing person to hunt for murderer.

I think the size thirteen is our man or one of them. I think he's a resident of Midnight Island or has easy access to it. I think he'll lay low now and wait us out because he's scared and won't make another move to expose himself. At least he won't if he's smart and I have no reason to believe that he isn't. I think a size-thirteen boot is pretty weak evidence and unless we're prepared to do a Cinderella, does-the-glass-slipper-fit search of every resident on the island and the county, it's a paper-thin slice of evidence to hang our hats on. Have I left anything out?"

"You don't consider the earring and blood spatter evidence?" Walt said.

"Possible motive for why he returned to the house, not for Amanda's disappearance," I said. "The two are related, but she wasn't kidnapped or killed over an earring and a few droplets of blood. They may give us a compass to the motive, but not a motive in itself."

"So how are you going to proceed?" Walt said.

"When Jane comes back I'm going to ask her to hold that press conference," I said. "She's going to state that she now has a strong person of interest and the investigation will proceed in that direction. Maybe he'll get spooked enough to slip up and expose himself again."

"You think that will work?"

"No."

Walt sighed. "If only the public knew how many murders and crimes in general go unresolved."

"They're better off not knowing," I said. "They're better off thinking everything gets solved in the sixty minutes it takes to watch an episode of their favorite cop show."

"I hate cop shows," Walt said.

"Yeah."

"Almost as much as I hate criminals," Walt said.

We finished our steaks. The sun was down and I built a fire

in the trashcan. I brewed a fresh pot of coffee and we sipped from mugs and watched the crackling fire in front of us.

"You know, John, sometimes the bad guy wins," Walt said.

"Yeah," I said.

"Where's Regan?"

"Oz took her and Mark to the movies."

"Janet?"

"She asked me not to call her and I haven't."

"Women," Walt said.

"Yeah," I said.

We were silent for a moment.

"So who has a key to the Felton house?" I said.

Walt looked at me.

"How many people have a key to your house?" I said.

"My wife and kids and me."

"You'd have to trust somebody a great deal to give them a key," I said. "Or let them get close enough to you to steal one. Either way it comes down to trust."

"Yeah," Walt said.

Seventeen

I spent a restless night in the bed, awoke early and went for a three-mile run along the beach just after sunrise. The salt sea air and run went a long way to removing the cobwebs from my mind and the kinks from my back.

Upon returning to the trailer, I drank the mug of coffee Regan gave me and puffed on the e-cigarette as I mulled things over for a bit.

I was convinced Amanda Felton was dead.

And that Size Thirteen was involved either as the murderer or someone close to him.

I had no idea what sparked Norman Felton's rampage on the Montero kid, but it had to be about Amanda because there was nothing else to assume. I had no idea what was behind Amanda Felton's disappearance/murder. But it was a safe bet to assume Size Thirteen thought the earring and blood were clues important enough to return to the house to find. I had no idea if the Montero kid was involved or just a witness in the wrong place at the wrong time. I knew Size Thirteen didn't leave Midnight Island after the attack on Jane and I didn't need to wait for Walt to get a rundown on the three cars that left on the ferry afterward. I knew that because he led me on a chase through the woods knowing exactly where he was going, how to double back and how to escape after attacking Jane. A visitor to the island would have simply gotten lost in the two square miles of thick woodlands.

I hadn't mentioned that to Jane or Walt yet. I wanted to play around with it a bit more before I was one hundred percent positive. And I had a reason for that. Midnight Island was a showplace of sorts and valuable real estate to the county in that many of the residents, year-round and snowbirds alike, paid huge amounts of property tax. If I made the hunt for Amanda's kidnapping/murder into a quest to find an island resident without a shred of proof other than a jog through the woods, every mayor and town manager in every town in the county would go nuts, including the county manager, tax assessor, public defenders and sitting judge.

To quote the late, great Jack Webb: Just the facts, ma'am.

And I didn't have one to grow on.

I finished the mug of coffee in my hand, then got up and went to the heavy bag beside the trailer. I slipped on the bag gloves and proceeded to pound the hundred-and-twenty-pound bag for thirty minutes.

Drenched in sweat, I tossed the gloves and got down on the hard sand and cranked out pushups until my chest burned and my arms gave out. I finished off with a few minutes of jumping rope on the sand and when there was nothing left in the tank I went in the trailer for a hot shower. While the hot needle spray washed away the exhaustion, I reviewed my thoughts that I had allowed to randomly pop in and out of my mind during the workout.

If Amanda Felton was dead as I now believed and her murderer was an island resident, as I now believed, how did the earring and blood tie into it?

Certainly the earring wasn't the murder weapon and the splatter of blood could have been caused by a simple slap to the nose or lip. And there was no proof that the lost earring and blood splatter happened at the same time.

So, why was the vacuum moved into the living room closet?

My guess was Size Thirteen thought the rug was cleaned of blood and the traces couldn't be detected.

My guess was he was there just for the earring.

Why?

The house had been gone over several times and the earring missed, so why risk discovery by going back for something nobody knew existed?

It was just dumb luck Size Thirteen picked the same day and time to return to the Felton house as we did. And where oh where did he get a key?

I turned off the shower and grabbed a towel just as my cell phone rang. I wrapped the towel around my waist and walked to the kitchen where the phone sat on the table. I checked the incoming number, pressed talk and said, "They let you out yet?"

"I'm on my way to the office," Jane said. "Anything new I should know about?"

"If by new you mean progress, the answer is no," I said.

"In the hospital overnight I had a lot of time to think," Jane said. "And the more I think about it, the more I have to see it as the girl is dead."

"I have that very same thought," I said. "Walt, too."

"What about today, what are you doing?"

"Thinking. You?"

"Do some of the stuff you mentioned. That press conference, check the patrol car in the Felton driveway."

"I'll check with you later."

I hung up, dressed quickly, and took the phone and fresh coffee out to my new lawn chair.

Paul Lawrence answered his own phone on the third ring. "No perky secretary screening your calls?" I said.

"We're on a tight budget these days," Lawrence said. "No room for perky."

"Do you have room for another favor?"

"Favors to you are like Jell-O, aren't they? Always room for more."

"I'm assuming nothing's developed on the missing persons home front?" I said.

"No hit on her description if that's what you mean."

"Can you do a nationwide search on Jane Does age twelve to eighteen?"

Lawrence was silent for a moment. "You've given up the idea she's alive?" he finally said.

"Closing in on three weeks," I said.

"I'll run it down and see what spits out," Lawrence said. "I was hoping this one would be the exception."

"She still might be, but it's doubtful," I said. "Either way, I'd like to find her and give her family some closure."

"Give me a few days," Lawrence said.

"Thanks, Paul."

I set the phone aside and sucked on the e-cigarette. I thought for a few moments and then went inside to fetch my car keys.

I stopped by Regan's room on the way out. She was reading a textbook of some kind. Molly was napping at the end of the bed.

"I have to go out for a bit," I said. "I'll ask Oz to come by and keep you company."

"Dad, I'm not eight," Regan said.

"I know, but Oz is and he gets lonely."

I pulled into the Felton driveway and parked next to the vacant cruiser. I grabbed a half-full water bottle, got out and started walking. I passed the back fence where Size Thirteen left his boot print and crossed the street to the woods.

I entered at the approximate spot where I'd followed Size Thirteen the day before and found the markings I'd made in the twigs and branches while running. The trail wasn't hard to follow. Two large men and one woman running through dense woods might as well leave a trail of breadcrumbs behind them.

I went several hundred yards and stopped at approximately the point where I'd heard him double back on my left flank. I turned left and walked until I found the path he'd carved out going back for Jane.

He was less than thirty yards from me that day when he backtracked. I followed his path until I reached the spot where he'd attacked Jane. The branch he used to knock Jane for a loop was still on the ground.

I picked up the branch. It had some heft to it, maybe four to five pounds. It was freshly ripped from a birch tree and that told me his intent was to make a weapon and use it, rather than a spur of the moment, panicky grab for the first object he spotted.

I held the branch and backtracked along the newly carved-out path. About thirty yards in I spotted a medium-sized birch tree with a busted limb. I held the branch to the limb. It was a spot-on match.

Size Thirteen must have feared he couldn't outrun me or reach the road undetected, broken off the branch to use as a weapon, and backtracked. The question in my mind was, did he know Jane was behind me and she was the target, or was I his target?

I returned to the point where Jane went down.

I studied the area for a moment. Size Thirteen had continued back the way he came after taking Jane down.

He wasn't after me. He knew Jane was behind me and in his way to a clear path to the road and escape.

I followed his trail past the point where we entered. He went about thirty yards more, then veered off to the right and back to the road.

I came out of the woods, stood on the soft shoulder and looked at the size-thirteen footprints in the dirt that led to the road. Did he have a car parked on the shoulder far enough away from the Felton home to avoid detection?

Or.

Did he jog from another point on the island to the Felton home and then run back to that point?

I searched the soft shoulder by the road. Not a tire track in sight or skid mark on the asphalt.

He jogged.

From a point on the island to the Felton home with a surprise detour through the woods and then back to his original point, where he did one of several things.

Retrieve his car, then drive to the ferry and off the island. The tapes from the bank said not likely.

Retrieve his car, hide out until it was safe to take the ferry, and cross over the next day. I made a mental note to ask Jane to have the ATM tapes for the day after the attack going forward one week sent to her office. It was possible Size Thirteen was staying at the hotel or one of a dozen or more bed-and-breakfast inns on the island and wasn't in a hurry to leave.

Jog back to the hotel, bed-and-breakfast or his home on the island.

It was noon when we arrived at the Felton home. Size Thirteen couldn't have gotten there much sooner because he didn't have time to do much else besides move the vacuum from one room to the closet of another.

I glanced at my watch. It was a bit after one in the afternoon and there wasn't a jogger or car on the road.

I started walking back to the Felton home. There wasn't a soul anywhere in sight, not in a yard, a window, a driveway or on the road. It stood to reason the majority of homeowners on the island were at work on the mainland.

So why jog when you could drive?

Cars make noise, and there is always the risk someone is home sick from work who hears the car and looks out the window. It might even be someone who recognizes you. They wave, you wave and you're remembered if and when somebody asks.

Jogging, though not as fast as driving, is silent. Silence is a main ingredient when planning to illegally enter someone's home in broad daylight.

Silence and a big damn key.

I reached the Felton driveway sight unseen, where I leaned against my car and puffed on the e-cigarette. One complete loop around the island was what, maybe seven and a half to eight miles, taking into account twists and turns on the road? At a slow jog I could complete one loop in around eighty-five minutes. At a run I could do it in around sixty to sixty-five minutes or so.

I got off my car and walked to the fence, stood level with it and eyeballed its height. I put it at an even seven-feet tall. Size Thirteen went up and over it like a jackrabbit and was in the woods by the time I reached the sidewalk.

Size Thirteen was athletic. A runner or jogger, a man capable of scaling a seven-foot high fence in a second or two, for whom jogging from Point A to the Felton home and back to Point A again wasn't much of a challenge.

Size Thirteen was a big man.

An athletic man.

And not afraid to get violent to save his skin.

I returned to my car and was about to get behind the wheel when Jane called me on my cell phone. "Bekker, I have Mr. Montero here in my office," Jane said. "He would like to meet with you as soon as possible."

"Impossible today," I said. "Meet with me about what?"

"He wants you to stay on this until the end," Jane said. "No matter what. He says he can afford to pay extra fees."

"What about his son?"

"No change as of this morning."

"How's his English?"

"Not as bad as I first thought."

"Where's he staying?"

"The hotel downtown, not far from the beach."

"Can you bring him by the trailer around seven-thirty?"

"I can do that."

"Ask him if he likes steak."

After hanging up with Jane, I got behind the wheel and smoked the damn e-cigarette while I mulled things over in my head.

Assuming the earring was Size Thirteen's reason for entering the house, how did he know one earring was missing from Amanda's ear that Saturday?

He would have to have been with her that Saturday to know that.

I stared at the yellow tape around the house.

Been with her why?

I pulled out my cell phone and called Jane back.

"Jane, your detectives checked all incoming and outgoing calls on the Felton home phone for the months prior; what did they find?" I said.

"Nothing of any use," Jane said. "Numbers called on a regular basis. His brother, neighbors—some of which we now know were babysitting customers—work, school; it all checks out. It's possible we missed something. Want us to pull phone bills from the phone company? They're more complete."

"I don't think so. What about his cell phone?"

"Work, school, home," Jane said. "Why? We covered this already."

"Amanda?"

"She didn't have a cell phone," Jane said. "Jack, we covered this already. What's going on with you?"

"Thinking out loud," I said. "Felton didn't have a home computer."

"No."

"Amanda?"

"Also, no. Bekker, we've . . ."

"Was she issued one from school?" I said. "Taking a course and needed one, something like that? It would be impossible to start high school without knowing how to use a computer."

Jane was silent for a moment.

"I'll have my detectives run out to the high school and check that out," she finally said.

"Thanks."

"Anything else? I still have Mr. Montero in my office."

"We'll talk about it later at my trailer," I said.

I set the phone on the seat next to me and closed my eyes.

For Size Thirteen to know Amanda was missing an earring, he would have had to be with her that Saturday.

Before or after Norman Felton left the house in a rage?

Say after.

Whatever caused Felton's rage was the reason Size Thirteen was called to the Felton home.

Guesswork for sure, but not improbable.

The same reason for Felton's rage caused Size Thirteen to strike Amanda, dislodging her earring and creating blood splatter.

More guesswork.

But not improbable.

Size Thirteen removed Amanda from the house for same reason as Felton's rage.

Size Thirteen doesn't notice the missing earring at the time.

He returns to the house to clean up the blood and thinks everything is fine until weeks later and returns again to find the missing earring.

Why?

And why wait weeks?

That didn't make sense.

Unless he believed the missing earring could link Amanda's disappearance to him. Then it made sense. Then it mattered.

How? By all accounts Amanda Felton was fine on Friday. What happened overnight that would cause her father to go on a rampage and lead to Size Thirteen's appearance on the scene, and Amanda's disappearance?

The earring?

Some dark secret.

A dark secret that Norman Felton found out about and went berserk over?

And after Felton left the house Amanda did what . . . call Size Thirteen? Phone records show that she didn't.

If she had a laptop issued by the school, could she have emailed somebody after her father left the house?

She could have.

For what reason?

I opened my eyes.

Why did Norman Felton rush to the high school that Saturday, leaving Amanda alone at home?

To confront somebody was the logical reason of choice.

Who?

Ubaldo Montero didn't fit. There was no evidence that Ubaldo Montero even knew Amanda Felton existed.

Whoever was shagging fly balls with Montero that Saturday could have been the target of Felton's rage and ran off at the sight of him, leaving Ubaldo to bear the brunt of his fury.

But who was the mystery person at the other end of those fly balls?

By all accounts Ubaldo had no interest in baseball. He played soccer back home. Maybe he wanted to learn the game to fit in with his peers? After tending to the field, he and a friend shag some baseballs around, take some batting practice to learn something new and bust a window in the process.

It fit.

But who was the friend?

Whoever was with Montero hadn't come forward. The entire school—hell, the entire state—knew about the incident by now and yet he'd kept silent.

What was his secret? How was it related to Felton's rage? How was it related to Amanda's disappearance?

I had no answers. It seemed the more I looked for answers, the more questions arose.

I looked at the Felton home. Deep in my gut I had the feeling Amanda Felton would never be seen or heard from again.

Cases like this one usually wind up on the news with a neighbor saying, "He was such a good boy," or, "He was a good neighbor, quiet and always kept to himself."

Yeah, right up to the moment he kidnapped a three year-old or cut your throat.

I glanced at my watch. It was time to go. I turned the key over in the ignition, backed out of the Felton driveway and drove back to the ferry.

I sucked on the e-cigarette and kept my speed to around thirty miles an hour on the narrow road to the center of town.

One missing girl.

One dead father.

One teenage boy in a coma.

One athletic jogger who knew his way around the island and wasn't afraid to use violence.

One missing earring.

A small amount of blood spatter.

Nothing to link anything together.

The same athletic jogger who thought the earring and blood spatter important enough evidence to risk returning to the Felton home for. Find the jogger and it all might fall into my lap.

Size Thirteen was the key to it all.

Thirteen.

Unlucky number.

Eighteen

The coals in my grill were reaching maximum temperature when Jane and Mr. Montero arrived at the trailer in Jane's cruiser.

Regan was visiting Mark at Clayton's condo. I told Clayton I wouldn't be able to pick her up until late, but he said she could stay over anytime she wanted.

Jorge Montero was a slight man in his late forties who could easily pass for sixty-five due to a lifetime of hard work under the hot Dominican sun. He wore a white shirt, tan slacks and a white skimmer hat from back home. His dark mustache was neatly trimmed.

Montero looked around at the trailer. "This is where you live?" he said in a thick accent.

I extended my right hand to him and we shook.

"I use this as my office," I said. "It's quiet and secluded. Please sit down."

Montero nodded and took a chair.

"I'll get the steaks on and then we can talk," I said.

I lifted the platter of steaks and tossed them onto the grill, and they made that satisfying sizzling sound so important to whetting the appetite.

"They say to me at the hospital my son may not wake up for a very long time," Montero said.

"I know," I said.

"They say to me the man who did this to my son has died,"

Montero said. "They say he maybe think my son is somebody else. They say the man's daughter is missing since that day and no one know why. They say you are looking for the girl and someone who may know why she disappeared. They say no one knows why Mr. Felton did what he did, but you suspect it is over his daughter."

I nodded. "They say a lot," I said. "By they, you mean Jane?"

"Yes, Sheriff Jane," Montero said.

I got up for a quick moment to flip the steaks and place the already-cooked baked potatoes on the grill to warm.

"Sheriff Jane tells me that you want to offer a reward for information about the missing girl even though Mr. Felton is dead," I said as I took my seat.

"Yes," Montero said. "And I'll pay you extra. Whatever you want."

"Why?" I said. "The man who attacked your son is dead. He can't be punished anymore."

"Somebody caused all this to happen," Montero said. "That somebody needs to pay for all this."

"I agree," I said. "We want the missing girl found even if she's no longer alive, and for me to do that I have to find that somebody you spoke of. I won't take your money, Mr. Montero, because I'm already getting paid."

Montero nodded and suddenly tears formed in his eyes. "My son is my life," he sniffled. "I can't lose him like this."

"I understand," I said. "Believe me, I do. Now I have some questions."

Montero nodded as he wiped his eyes.

"Your son played soccer back home, but did he ever express interest in baseball?" I said.

"Your baseball is very popular back home, but not like what you call soccer," Montero said. "He played soccer but everybody does. He was more interested in school, in college. He wanted to study physics at university."

"How often did he call and write home?" I said.

"He call two times a week," Montero said.

"Did he talk about school, friends, a girlfriend, things like that?"

"About school, his grades and sometimes friends," Montero said. "And his foster family. I speak with them yesterday and again today. They are very nice, very good people. They are very upset about all this."

"Many people are," I said. "I think our steaks are done."

The moon was high and bright and full when we took a walk down the beach after dinner. We left our shoes and socks at the trailer and with rolled-up pants, we walked along the shore in ankle-deep water.

"It's very nice here," Montero said. "Even if the water is a bit cold."

"Mr. Montero, how long is your visa stay?" I said.

"One month."

"That's quite a bill," I said. "Travel, hotel, food and reward."

Montero nodded. "I have my savings," he said.

"Jane, is there a cheaper motel near the hospital where Mr. Montero can stay for a while?"

"One with a pool a few blocks away," Jane said.

"You could walk to visit your son," I said.

Montero nodded, wiped his eyes and looked at me. "Why?" he finally said.

I looked at Jane. "We'll do everything we can to answer that question."

I was alone in my chair with my thoughts. I started a bonfire in the trashcan and sipped coffee and puffed on the e-cigarette for a while.

The world can sometimes be an ugly and frightening place.

That's because some of the people in it are ugly and frightening, and make it so.

Jane was right in her analogy that Norman Felton and I had something in common.

Inside each and every one of us is a locked-away rage that most of us never acknowledge. It's under control and we never have to look at it in the mirror. It's there, though, below the surface of what we call civilized society.

Locked away.

Ticking.

Ugly.

Fearsome.

Waiting.

That day I came home and found Carol dead and Regan a vegetable, I lost all control. I was told it took a group of uniformed officers to put me down, I was in such a rage. Had Carol's murderer been in front of me at that moment, I would have killed him on the spot. I would have beaten him to death and even after he was dead I would have kept pounding his lifeless body until it was a mass of bloody jelly.

That's that place below the surface of what we call civilized society.

Norman Felton went there that day.

I knew exactly how he felt and what he thought.

Kill whoever hurt his daughter.

Once that train starts rolling it has to be derailed in order to stop it. You can't talk it down or reason with it. You can't make it change direction. You can only pull the tracks from under the wheels and crash it into a wall.

What brought that out in Norman Felton?

His wife was gone seven years. Someone hurt his daughter.

What do you do to a fourteen-year-old girl that could set a

man off like that?

Sex.

Or drugs.

Or both.

By all accounts Amanda Felton was not involved with drugs. By all accounts Amanda Felton didn't have a boyfriend.

I puffed on the e-cigarette and sat in silence with my thoughts. After a while I picked up my cell phone and called Jane.

"I just dropped Montero off at the motel," Jane said. "It's two blocks to the hospital."

"Jane, tomorrow morning make some calls," I said.

"To who and about what?" Jane said.

"Check with hospitals, Planned Parenthood and medical clinics in the state for girls Amanda's age who might have come in for treatment for the possibility of rape," I said.

"Already did that," Jane said. "Nothing."

"Then check them for abortions," I said.

Jane was dead silent for a very long moment.

"It would make me pick up a bat," I said.

NINETEEN

"Mr. Felton, I know the words are harsh and don't go down easy, but the probability is high and I need to know everything and anything about your brother and Amanda," I said.

We were in Felton's office at Felton Motors, he behind his desk, me in a chair opposite it.

Felton was choked up to the point he needed a minute. He must have had the same thoughts about Amanda as the words I just spoke to him, but sometimes hearing the words can bring out emotions thoughts can't.

This was one of those times.

"I know that it's probably true," Felton said. "But . . . I think in the back of my mind I was hoping it wasn't. Sorry for my breakdown."

"Don't apologize for loving your niece," I said. "As the father of a young woman I know exactly how you feel. My question stands, though."

Felton nodded. "This man, the one you call Size Thirteen, is the only suspect?"

"So far," I said. "But he's a good one. He had a key and was there for a purpose that day, and I doubt it was to borrow the vacuum."

"So it shouldn't be that hard to catch him?" Felton said.

"It will be damn near impossible," I said.

Felton looked his question at me.

"He knows he got away by sheer luck," I said. "He also knows the sheriff's department, local and state police, and FBI are in on the game. He will lay low, very low, do nothing to attract attention and try to fade away."

"And the police can do nothing about it?" Felton said.

"Even if he lives on the island there are hundreds of potential suspects," I said. "And if he doesn't we're talking tens of thousands. No cop is going to ask a judge for search warrants based only upon size-thirteen feet."

"So he gets away with murder," Felton said.

"I didn't say that," I said. "What I am saying is this could drag on for quite a long time before he does something that gives me a break."

"You said 'me,' " Felton said. "Not 'us.' "

"Sometimes I work better alone," I said. "And I don't worry about search warrants or court orders."

Felton nodded. "All right," he said.

"So put on your thinking cap and try to remember everything you can that might be helpful," I said. "Conversations with Amanda and Norman that at the time seemed meaningless, things like that. I'll call you in a day or two. All right?"

Felton nodded.

The intercom on his desk buzzed. Felton pushed a button and a salesman said, "Mr. Felton, Mr. Bekker's daughter would like him in the showroom."

I nodded.

"He'll be right there," Felton said.

I stood up.

"I'll go with you," Felton said. "I'll make this one my paper and take a loss."

I said, "Let her haggle, but no special treatment. I want her to learn life isn't free."

"You sure?"

I nodded.

Regan sat opposite the salesman at his desk. She turned to look at me and Felton when we left his office and entered the showroom.

"Dad," Regan said.

"How'd we do?" I said.

"I knocked the price down to seventeen-one from seventeen-four, and that includes the two-year warranty and added features," the salesman said.

Felton looked at Regan. "Sound fair to you, young lady?"

Regan, still shy around strangers in social situations, nodded meekly.

"Tell you what," Felton said. "I'll toss in another two years on the warranty, no charge. Fair?"

I nodded to Regan and she smiled.

"Why don't you finish up the paperwork while I talk to Mr. Felton," I said.

I lit a cigarette behind the showroom office and looked at Felton.

"Thanks for the extra years," I said.

"No problem," Felton said. "Glad to help. She's a beautiful girl."

"She looks like her mother," I said.

We were silent for a moment.

"All week I've tried to remember things, things that might be important," Felton said. "Something that might be useful to you."

"Old cop trick," I said. "Sometimes when you're looking for something really big you got to look at something really small first."

Felton looked at me and slowly nodded.

I shook his hand. "Talk to you soon," I said.

I leaned into the window of the Marquis and said, "See you at home."

Oz nodded from behind the wheel. "I get forty cents a mile for playing Driving Miss Daisy, right?"

"This was a business trip, wasn't it?" I said.

"Hot damn, I can buy me that dream house now," Oz said.

"Who's Miss Daisy?" Mark said, next to Oz.

"Never mind and buckle your seat belt," I said.

"How much does the passenger get per mile?" Mark said. "Seeing as how I gotta listen to him the next four hours."

"You get paid in the wisdom of my company," Oz said.

I left the Marquis and crossed the lot where Regan was behind the wheel of her Impala. Regan was buckled up, hands on the wheel so tight her knuckles were pale.

I got in beside her.

"Are you ready, hon?" I said.

Regan looked at me. Her face had the color of bleached flour.

"I'm afraid," she said. "It was different driving your car."

"At least with your car you won't have to stick your feet down the floorboard hole and pedal to start," I said. "All you have to do is turn the key."

And she did.

Yabba Dabba Doo.

TWENTY

Late in the afternoon, Jane came by the trailer with some news. I was shirtless, in the middle of a heavy-bag workout, when I heard her cruiser pull up and the door close.

"Jesus, Bekker," Jane said when she came around the side of the trailer where I was pounding the bag. "Don't you ever get tired of that shit?"

I lowered my hands, removed the gloves and tossed them to the sand beside the bag. "Want some coffee?" I said.

"Yeah."

We went around to the front of the trailer where I went inside, tossed on a tee shirt and filled two mugs with coffee from the pot I'd made a little while ago. Jane was in a chair, smoking a cigarette when I came out and took my seat. I passed her a mug.

"Thanks," Jane said.

"What did you find out?" I said.

Jane sipped, drew on the cigarette, exhaled and said, "It's impossible to determine if Amanda Felton called a Planned Parenthood or another clinic. They have no record of her name on file and they get a hundred hang-ups a week from girls who call and lose their nerve."

"And no way to trace her calls if she did make one from a pay phone and hang up?" I said.

"No."

I sipped some coffee, set the mug down on the card table and grabbed my smokes. "Something I've been mulling over," I said. "Size Thirteen: why was he wearing boots that day? We didn't find evidence of a car parked nearby, which tells us he walked from Point A to Point B. At first I thought he might have jogged to the Felton home from Point B, but if that was his plan, why boots and not comfortable jogging shoes?"

"Maybe he wasn't planning to jog?" Jane said. "Maybe he figured a walk from Point B to the Felton home would be no big deal."

"Know what I think?" I said. "At first I thought he jogged to keep from calling attention to a car pulling into the Felton driveway. But nobody jogs in boots. I think he used the woods as cover to go from Point A to Point B. Hiking boots for a hike through the woods."

"He'd have to be very familiar with those woods to do that," Jane said.

"Like a permanent resident familiar," I said.

"Make an island resident the person of interest and only potential suspect, nobody is going to like that," Jane said. "The taxes those people pay support ten percent of the county."

"The hell with taxes," I said. "It fits and that's more important."

"It fits, but without a name, a person, a scrap of evidence to prove this, I can't make a public statement saying we think it's an island resident behind this whole mess."

"I'm not asking you to," I said. "Besides, our man is so far buried he's never going to stick his head out. Public statement wouldn't do a bit of good."

"What would?"

"If he waltzed into your office and confessed in front of the media to kidnapping and murdering Amanda Felton," I said.

Jane grinned. "Do they ever really do that?"

"Happens all the time in the movies," I said.

Jane's cell phone rang and she pulled it from her belt. "Morgan," she said.

I went inside to touch up my mug while Jane was on the phone. When I came back out, she had returned the phone to her belt and was standing.

"Gotta go?" I said.

"Yeah."

"I think my theory of Size Thirteen is solid."

"Me, too. Question is what do we do next?"

"Don't know. Wish I did."

Jane nodded. "See ya, Bekker."

"Yup."

I watched Jane return to her cruiser and drive off the beach. I finished my coffee and returned to the heavy bag. I slipped on the gloves and warmed up again with some jabs.

Hiking boots.

For a hike in the woods.

I worked in a few left hooks.

Two miles long and a half mile wide of deep woodlands. Easy to get lost in, get turned around in unless . . .

I switched from left hooks to straight rights and three-punch combinations.

. . . You knew the woods and were comfortable hiking in them. You leave Point A, travel in the woods at a leisurely pace sight unseen, and emerge at the Felton home.

Yeah.

I worked in some body blows, hard lefts and stiff jabs.

Like I told Jane, it fit.

I switched back to the jab and hit the bag one hundred times.

It would fit better with a suspect.

I went from jabs to left hooks and drove my fist into the bag another one hundred times or so.

A suspect with size-thirteen boots and a key.

I switched to right hooks and dug in for another hundred punches.

And a reason.

I lowered my arms to my sides. Sweat poured off me like rain drops.

I went back around, stripped off the gloves, tossed them on the card table and took a seat in my lawn chair.

Even when there is nothing on the surface and nothing below it, there is always a reason why something happens.

John Dillinger, the famous bank robber from the thirties, once told a reporter when he was asked why he robbed banks, "Because that's where the money is." Old John knew what he was talking about.

Yeah.

I went inside for a mug of coffee, sat and sucked on the e-cigarette for a bit. Regan and Oz were in the municipal parking lot adjacent to the beach where he was teaching her the finer points of parallel parking. I hadn't checked my cell phone most of the day, and when I looked there was a message from a cell phone with an area code for Hawaii.

I hit the call button and after three rings, Joey said, "Is that you, Mr. Bekker?"

"It is and call me Jack," I said. "That's what my friends call me."

"Okay, Jack it is," Joey said. "So I'm in New York at the hospice. My parents are at a hotel over on Fifth Avenue. I start treatment tomorrow. I had meetings all day with the doctors and they seem optimistic about my recovery."

"Me, too," I said.

"So . . . what I was wondering is . . . do you come to New York at all?" Joey said.

"Not a lot, no."

"Oh."

"So maybe I'm due for a visit," I said.

"Really?"

"Why not?" I said. "End of the week maybe if you're up for it. Those first treatments can be pretty rough. Ask your doctors and if they agree I'll pop on over."

"That would be good," Joey said. "My dad has to fly back to Hawaii in a few days for some court case and my mom . . . she's not much fun to be around."

"I'm sure this is a great strain on her," I said. "I'm sure when this is over and she's relieved, you might just see her in a new light."

"You think?"

"Yes."

"Someone's coming, a nurse I think," Joey said.

"Call me in a few days and let me know about a visit," I said. "I'll bring you a surprise."

"I'd like that," Joey said.

After I hung up with Joey I sat in the chair for a while and decided a trip to town was in order. I hadn't bought anything new for myself in quite a while and could use a nice pair of hiking boots.

TWENTY-ONE

I joined Regan and Oz at the patio table for a breakfast of French toast with cinnamon, butter and syrup and bacon on the side.

"Why are you dressed like a park ranger, Dad?" Regan said between bites of toast.

"These are work clothes," I said. "And the reason is I'll be outdoors most of the day, and if they get ripped who cares?"

"Outdoors where?" Regan said.

"Midnight Island," I said as I grabbed a few pieces of French toast and bacon. "I'm not sure how long I'll be gone. What are you doing today?"

"Practicing parallel parking and my stop signs," Regan said. "Oz says my parking won't pass the exam and I roll stop signs."

I dumped melted butter and syrup over the toast and bacon.

"It's because I'm short," Regan said. "When I parallel park I can't see. Mom was like five-ten and you're John Wayne–tall, so why am I short?"

"Good things come . . ." I said.

"In small packages," Regan said. "Yeah, I know. But small packages can't see over the hood of a car."

I parked the Marquis in the lot on the Midnight Island ferry dock just after ten in the morning. Before getting out, I opened the glove box for the Sig .380 pistol and extra seven-round clip I keep there for just such occasions. On the seat next to me was a stainless-steel water bottle with carabiner belt clip.

I exited my car, stuck the Sig in the small of my back under my shirt and clipped the water bottle to a right-side belt loop.

I walked a block down Main Street past the hotel and made a right turn to where the fringe of woods acted as a starting point. At one time the entire island must have been nothing but woodlands, before it was settled and populated. According to the maps I'd studied of the island, about two and a half miles of woods stretched out before me, a half mile wide at its widest.

Plenty of room to get lost in.

Or hide in.

I stayed close to the street, maybe fifty feet in, and walked at a moderate pace. After a half mile a path became clear and I followed it for another half mile to the point where the Felton home was located.

I kept walking. The path forked, but I stayed with the one I was on and walked it to the very end where the woods ended with the hairpin turn.

I came out and stood on the road.

I could see the Stewart home and Crawford home opposite the woods just before the turn. Not that it meant a thing, but they were the only two homes of the five families Amanda baby-sat for that faced the woods.

My hike proved fruitless in that I learned nothing new, uncovered no startling piece of evidence or even a remote link to anything.

I unclipped the water bottle from my belt loop and took a few sips, then clipped it back on and thought for a moment. Then I decided to take the return trip along the road.

I walked a mile or so and stopped at the Felton home. Jane's cruiser was undisturbed in the driveway. The yellow crime tape was intact. I stood in the driveway and stared at the house for a while.

I sipped some water.

I puffed on the e-cigarette a few times.

I let my thoughts flow and ebb at random.

Maybe Size Thirteen came from the other side of the Island? Maybe he didn't hike along a trail, but cut straight through from one side to the other?

About a half mile?

How long could that take, even in woods?

I turned and faced the woods.

A half mile to the other side. I checked my watch, entered the woods and started walking. I cut a path to the other side and emerged on the road twenty-seven minutes later.

Twenty-seven minutes to complete a slow walk through a half mile of thick woodlands. Size Thirteen easily could have done the same thing, although I saw no signs of a trail along the way.

I decided to walk back along the road to the ferry. After a quarter mile or so, I passed the Barrett home. A car was in their driveway.

I traveled the remaining mile or so along the road and arrived at the ferry point with a twenty-minute wait for the next boat back to the mainland. I ducked into the deli across the street from the hotel and picked up a coffee and a lemon Danish.

I ate and drank in my car while I waited for the ferry.

My morning's work produced nothing except some sweat on the back of my neck. When the ferry arrived, I drove my car across the bridge onto the boat and parked. I got out and stood along the railing to watch the ocean.

As the ferry pulled away from the dock, I turned to look at the island. Besides me there were just one or two other passengers heading to the mainland. A crew member to the captain walked past me on his way below.

"Excuse me," I said. "I have a question."

The assistant paused. "Sure."

"I noticed there are no private docks or public boat launches on the island," I said. "I was wondering why."

"Rocky coast," the assistant said. "Zoning laws and all that. If you're an island resident and own a boat you have to dock it on the mainland."

"Thanks."

I stared out at the ocean before me. In the distance I could see the coastline of the mainland.

Size Thirteen, if he lived on the mainland, didn't take a private boat to the island. If he drove and rode the ferry, he didn't ride it back the day we encountered him at the Felton home.

I was convinced he lived on the island.

Now all I needed was a link to Amanda Felton's disappearance, her father's violent tirade, the missing earring and Ubaldo Montero, and I was all set.

Open and shut.

Except I was on fumes and there wasn't a gas station in sight.

The mainland was coming closer and I was about to return to my car when my cell phone rang. Oz.

"Bekker, you better come home," he said.

"I am. What's up?"

"She lost an earring," Oz said. "The pair you gave her from Hawaii. She's tearing up the car looking for it and crying up a storm."

"Where are you?"

"Parking lot off the beach."

"Keep her calm," I said. "Don't let her get out of control whatever you do. I'm on my way."

Twenty minutes later I came up behind Regan's Impala. Oz was standing beside it with a worried look on his face. I parked and walked to the driver's side door, opened it and got in beside my daughter.

Regan flung herself against my chest and started crying.

I stroked her hair.

"It's okay," I said. "I'm here."

I let Regan cry herself out and when she was dry, I took her by the shoulders and said, "So what happened? Tell me."

"We were practicing parking," Regan said. "I turned my head and noticed in the mirror that my left earring was gone. I had them both at breakfast. It was the first thing I did when I got up this morning was put them on."

"Not in the car?" I said.

"No."

"They can be replaced," I said.

"It won't be the same," Regan said. "They were a gift from you. I don't care if they are real or not, you gave them to me and I lost one. The next thing I know I was crying and trying to rip out the seat."

"You had an anxiety attack," I said.

"Why?"

"Anxiety," I said.

"That's a big help."

"I don't know why, not really," I said. "I wasn't sober all that much when you were younger."

Regan rolled her eyes at me in frustration.

"Maybe you'd like to talk with Father Tomas and Sister Mary?" I said.

Father Tomas, the director of Hope Springs Eternal, was also Regan's psychiatrist for the decade that she spent under his care. Sister Mary Martin, his assistant, became the older sibling Regan never had.

Regan nodded. "I miss them."

"I'm sure they miss you."

"I'm okay now."

"Let's go home and I'll call Father Tomas."

"Okay."

I sat with Sister Mary Martin at the backyard patio table at Hope Springs Eternal while Father Tomas spoke with Regan in his office. We had mugs of coffee. I resisted the strong temptation to puff on the e-cigarette in front of the nun, although I doubt she would have objected.

"Frankly, I'm surprised she hasn't had more episodes like this one," Sister Mary Martin said. "She's come a long way in a short time, but the wound is still open and she's quite young and vulnerable."

I took a sip from my mug.

"Couple that with fear of losing her aunt if you two break up more than likely overwhelmed her and led to the anxiety attack," Sister Mary Martin said. "The lost earring was simply a trigger."

I nodded.

"How are you doing?" Sister Mary Martin said.

"My best," I said.

The nun sipped some coffee and nodded at me. "Mr. Bekker, may I offer some advice?"

"Sure."

"Regan may be nineteen now and give the appearance of being a confident young woman, but in many ways she is still very young and inexperienced. She has a lot of catching up to do in the emotional department, if you understand my meaning."

"I do," I said.

Sister Mary Martin took a sip of coffee. "Good."

The door to the garden slid open. Regan and Father Tomas came out and joined us at the table. "We had a nice chat," Father Tomas said.

I looked at Regan.

"I told Regan to call or come see me as often as she wishes," Father Tomas said. "And not to wait until things get all bottled up inside."

"I promise," Regan said.

Sister Mary Martin hugged and kissed Regan. "I'm always just a call away," she said.

I looked at my daughter. "Ready to go home?"

"Yes."

"Wanna stop for ice cream?"

"I'm not a baby, Dad," Regan chided me.

"Good, then you can drive," I said and tossed her the car keys. "And I still want to stop for ice cream."

"Okay, but no pistachio," Regan said and stuck her tongue out at me. "That's for little kids."

"I like pistachio," I said.

"Need I say more?"

TWENTY-TWO

"How important are real earrings to a woman?" I said.

Jane turned in her chair and looked at me. "By real you mean diamonds? And the pair you brought her back from Hawaii?"

"Yes."

"To answer your question, how important is a penis to a man?" Jane said.

"I don't get it," I said.

"Usually a woman does not buy herself diamond earrings," Jane said. "She receives them as a gift and usually from someone very close. Her father or husband, and it usually marks a special occasion. Same with a ring, such as an engagement ring. More than the diamonds, it's the emotion of receiving them from someone special that makes it a treasure."

I looked at Jane. Her blond hair and fair skin glowed from the light from the trashcan bonfire.

"I'm more than a pretty face, you know," she said.

I nodded.

She lit a real cigarette. I puffed on the fake one.

"This isn't about the earrings you gave Regan, is it?" Jane said.

"No."

"Amanda Felton?"

"Yes."

Some gulls started fighting down at the surf, probably over scraps of food.

"I got to go home," Jane said. "These eighteen-hour days are killing me."

"What time do you want to meet in the morning?"

"Ten."

Jane nodded.

"So go get some sleep," I said.

Jane looked at me. "I'm tired, Jack," she said. "I've had my fill of the job. Next election I'm not running. I'm going to retire, collect my pension and take up knitting."

"Do you know how to knit?" I said.

"I use a stapler to fix a torn pocket," Jane said. "See you in the morning."

I waited for the taillights on Jane's cruiser to disappear off the beach before I stood up from my chair. Out of the corner of my eye I saw Molly in the shadows, rolling around in the sand.

"What are you doing out here?" I said. After Regan went to bed I left the door open and the little cat had wandered outside to check things out.

Molly looked at me. Her eyes glowed yellow in the light of the dying bonfire.

She had something in her mouth, and flipped it and caught it with her paw.

"What have you got there?" I said.

I knelt down beside Molly and she looked at me. Regan's missing earring glinted in the light from the bonfire.

I lifted Molly in my arms and removed the earring from her paw.

I scratched her ears. "I don't suppose you could find the backer?" I said.

I brought Molly and the earring inside and closed the door.

Regan always slept with the door open and the nightlight on. She was asleep on her side when I quietly entered her bedroom and set Molly on the bed beside her.

"Regan?" I said, softly.

She turned, opened her eyes and looked at me. "Dad?"

"Molly was tossing this around like a softball," I said and held out the earring. "I thought you might want it back."

I leaned up against the railing of the ferryboat and puffed on the e-cigarette while Jane flaunted the real one she smoked in my face. We stood side-by-side and watched the mainland grow smaller in the distance.

"What kind of earrings do you wear?" I said.

"None when I'm on duty, which is eighty percent of the time it seems," Jane said.

"What did you wear to Walt's promotion?"

"Pearls to match the necklace I wore."

"From your husband?"

"Right," Jane said. "Like the cheap bastard would part with a nickel that he couldn't eat, swing a club at or ride. No, I bought them myself as a treat to wear to Walt's party. But I do know where you're coming from. I still have the earrings my dad gave me the day I graduated high school."

The ferry changed direction and swung around in a new course to the docking bay on the island. The morning sun lit up the tree line to a bright emerald green.

"Marilyn got it right when she said diamonds are a girl's best friend, especially if they came from Daddy," Jane said. She flicked her cigarette overboard.

"My idiot husband is having an affair with a twenty-four-year-old that cuts his hair at that place in the mall," she said. "I found a receipt from a motel and spoke to the desk clerk who checked him and the bimbo in. It wasn't the first time."

"I'm really sorry," I said. "What are you going to do about it?"

Jane reached for her pack and withdrew the last cigarette.

She crumpled the pack and tossed it into the open window of her cruiser. Then she lit the cigarette, blew smoke and looked at me.

"Funny, but I thought I would be a lot more mad than I am," she said. "Thing is, I'm not even mad at all. Even after talking to the desk clerk at that motel. Even after driving to the mall to check out Miss Snip-snip's fake boobs, I'm not in the least bit goddamn mad. What is it with you men and boobs anyway, huh?"

Jane inhaled on the cigarette and blew twin streams of smoke out through her nose.

"So what are you going to do?" I said.

"Let him have Miss Wash and Dry, put in my papers before the next election and then . . . I don't know," Jane said.

I stretched out my arm around her shoulder and she placed her arm around my waist.

"Aren't we just a couple of stupid people," Jane said.

"You can tell that by what we do for a living," I said.

"Oh shut up," Jane said. "Asshole," she added.

I put a pot of coffee on to brew while Jane and I searched Amanda Felton's bedroom once again. If we'd missed something the first time, we missed it again. We picked up her jewelry box, designed to hold necklaces in a cabinet with French doors and rings and earrings in two pull-out drawers below the doors.

"Let's do this in the backyard," I said.

Armed with mugs of coffee, a notepad and the jewelry box, we took seats at the patio table. "What exactly are we looking for, Bekker?" Jane said.

"A feeling in my gut," I said.

"Tums usually work on that."

Behind the French doors were several dozen necklaces of the ten- to twelve-dollar variety usually found at the accessories store in any mall across the country. Same for bracelets and hair scrunchies.

We made an inventory of all necklaces, bracelets and hair scrunchies before opening the earring drawers. Amanda had a total of thirty-seven pairs of earrings. Eleven pairs were of the clip-on type.

"Before she got her ears pierced," Jane said.

"How old you figure?" I said.

"I was eight or nine," Jane said. "She was probably the same."

All thirty-seven pairs of earrings were little more than costume jewelry. One pair caught my eyes and I held up one earring to Jane. "What's this?"

"Cubic zirconium," Jane said. "Fake diamonds."

"Worth?"

"Maybe twenty-nine bucks at the mall. You don't know a lot about woman's stuff, do you?"

"Not enough to fill an eye dropper. Does it look familiar at all to you?"

Jane took the earring and gave it a once-over. "Looks a lot like the real diamond one we found in the living room," she said.

"It does, doesn't it?"

"But it's not. It's junk jewelry."

"I know," I said. "Mark it down I'm taking this pair."

"Why?"

"The feeling in my gut tells me to do so," I said. "And I haven't been to the mall since . . . ever."

"When you go to the mall, bring some Tums," Jane suggested.

Turns out there are three malls with nine jewelry stores in them and more than a dozen free-standing jewelry stores in town and the suburbs.

Oz and Regan were watching an instructional DVD about

parallel parking on television when I entered the trailer. I grabbed some coffee from the pot and took a seat. "Where did the DVD come from?"

"Borrowed it from my brother," Oz said.

"I need to borrow my daughter for a while."

Regan looked at me.

"I have to go shopping," I said. "To the mall."

"Can we take my car?" Regan said. "It's just sitting there doing nothing."

"Sure, but can you change and make yourself look younger?"

Regan glared at me. "Younger than what, Dad? I barely look fourteen as it is."

"Have you lost what's left of your mind?" Oz said. "The girl looks good just the way she is."

"She looks like an adult," I said.

"I do?" Regan said. "Since when?"

"Since now and go downsize," I said.

"Gimme ten minutes," Regan said.

Regan drove her Impala to our first stop, the mall closest to the house. She wore loose fitting jeans, a white tee shirt a dozen sizes too large that she'd ripped off from my dresser, a baseball cap and for good measure, painted her fingernails hot pink with little stars. How she got the stars on her nails was a mystery to me that would remain unsolved.

"Anything in particular you want me to do or say?" Regan asked as she parked in a spot twenty rows deep at the mall.

"Act young and follow my lead," I said. "And wear one earring."

Regan removed the baseball cap, put her hair in a ponytail and poked the end of it out the back adjustable hole in the cap.

"How do I look?" Regan said.

"Like a twelve-year-old boy," I said and gave her the earring that belonged to Amanda Felton.

"Marvelous," Regan said and handed the earring back to me.

I'd briefed Regan on the drive. I explained to her that my interest in a pair of kiddy earrings wouldn't appear so strange to the sales staff if my young daughter was with me in the store.

"Just follow my lead," I said as we entered the mall.

"Am I getting paid for this?"

"I'll buy you another ice cream cone," I said.

Regan smirked. "Big spender."

The first jewelry store was a cookie-cutter type located just off the food court. A male/female team of sales clerks was on duty. The female approached me when she saw Regan on my arm. "Good afternoon," the clerk said in a cheery voice.

"Why don't you go look around, honey," I told Regan.

"Okay, Dad," Regan said in a twelve-year-old voice.

"I've got a dad problem," I said. "I know my little girl doesn't look it, but she's fifteen and just started high school. Anyway, last summer they had the graduation dance when she graduated eighth grade, and she went to the prom or whatever you call it with a boy, and he gave her a pair of earrings. Well, I broke one of them and she's very upset about it. Funny thing, she doesn't even talk to that boy anymore, but I guess it's like a keepsake or something."

"Did you bring the memento?"

"The . . . oh, the earring," I said. "Yes I did."

I dug an earring out from my jacket pocket and gave it to the saleswoman. She held it up, gave it a once-over and handed it back to me.

"It's not one of ours," she said.

"Are you sure?"

She nodded. "Positive. I'm sorry. Try one of the other stores in the mall."

★ ★ ★ ★ ★

We left the mall after striking out at all three stores, and Regan drove us nine miles east to the next mall on my list.

"You have a fun job," Regan commented.

"A regular barrel of monkeys," I said.

"What's fun about a barrel of monkeys?" Regan said. "I think it would be loud, crowded and smell real bad. Kinda like your car."

"Never mind my car," I said. I started tapping my fingers against the dashboard.

"No," Regan said.

"No, what?"

"You'll just have to wait until we get to the next mall to smoke your e-cigarette. I know it's only vapor, but you're being weaned."

I quit tapping my fingers. "I am?"

The next mall proved as fruitless as the first. We pushed on to mall number three.

"What if they don't have them at the next mall?" Regan said.

"Then we hit the free-standing stores in the morning," I said.

In the second jewelry store in the third mall, a saleswoman smiled at me and said, "I wondered who the lucky girl was Jimmy was giving these to."

"Jimmy?" I said. "Oh, you mean James?"

"The Crawford boy," the woman said. "Ya gotta be a football hero and all that. So where is the lucky girl?"

"She's . . . well, she was right here," I said.

Regan came out from behind a mirrored post. The baseball cap was gone, her hair was down and a touch of gloss glistened on her lips. A wide belt around her waist made the too-large tee shirt look like a tunic top over the jeans.

"She's adorable," the saleswoman said.

I looked at Regan.

Regan gave me a tiny smirk.

"That's them," Regan said as the saleswoman showed her the earrings.

"I'm sorry, but I can't sell just one. They're a set," the saleswoman said.

"No problem," I said.

As we crossed the food court to the parking lot, Regan said, "I think you owe me a smoothie."

"I think you're right," I said.

The perimeter of the mall was lined with benches, trees and there was even a tiny garden off the food court with some shaded tables. We took our smoothies to a table in the shade.

"Who's Jimmy Crawford?" Regan said.

"James," I said. "He hates to be called Jimmy, remember."

Regan sucked in some smoothie, swallowed and said, "James, then."

"He's none of your concern and that was a pretty neat trick you pulled back there going from twelve to twenty," I said.

"I came prepared," Regan said. "I figured you would need the help, being a major klutz and all."

"I did. Thanks." I glanced around at the other tables.

"Go on if you must," Regan said.

I pulled out my electronic smoke and fed my addiction. "So listen," I said. "I'm thinking we won't mention this to anybody."

"Mention what, that you took me, Oz and Mark out to dinner at that fancy steak house by the ocean tonight?" Regan said.

"Yeah, that," I said.

Twenty-Three

Walt sunk his teeth into a still warm Boston cream donut from Pat's, made a noise of contentment, and then washed it down with a sip of Pat's coffee. "It's thin," he said when his throat was clear.

Jane selected a giant coffee roll, also still warm. "Thin doesn't mean it isn't true or condemning," she said and bit off a T-Rex sized hunk of roll.

I had a lemon cream. "Do you think it's coincidence that the Crawford boy bought a pair of the same earrings Amanda Felton owned and she just happens to babysit his kid sister?" I dunked the lemon cream into my coffee and took a bite.

"No, I don't," Walt said. "But no judge is going to hear evidence based on a pair of junk earrings you have no proof he gave to the Felton girl. They're a common type of junk jewelry and he could have given them to any young girl in the state."

"Who said anything about a judge?" I said.

After tossing back the last bit of Boston cream, Walt eyed the Pat's box on the card table. "What else you got in there?"

"A dozen or so more," I said.

Walt flipped open the box and removed a glazed donut dripping with honey.

"I wanted that one," Jane said.

"There's two," Walt said.

"I need more," I said. "I know that. But it's a lot more than we had yesterday."

Walt bit into his honey donut and washed it down with coffee. "Jane, what do you think?" he said. "It's your case."

Reaching into the Pat's box, Jane said, "It's too coincidental to be coincidence."

"What the hell's that mean?" Walt said.

"It's the first real link to the Felton girl and anybody," Jane said. "Thin or not, I think Bekker's on to something worth looking at."

Walt eyed me. "I do, too, the son of a bitch."

I polished off the lemon cream and sipped coffee. "I can tell you this much," I said. "Norman Felton didn't go off half-crazed and beat the Montero kid with a bat over some costume jewelry the Crawford boy may or may not have given Amanda Felton."

Jane reached into the box for the other honey donut.

"It's never easy, is it?" Walt said.

"That's why God gave us donuts, to soothe us over the rough spots," I said.

"God gave us donuts, huh?" Walt said.

I grabbed my e-cigarette and happily puffed away.

"So what now?" Walt said.

"I stay with it, see where it goes," I said. "Or doesn't go."

"Alone?" Walt said and eyed Jane.

"The sheriff's department is still running this investigation, Walt," Jane said.

"I know," Walt said. "Who's running Jack?"

"Walt, we go back almost thirty years," I said. "If you got something to say to me, come right out and say it."

"All right," Walt said. "You're the best goddamn cop I've ever seen. Better than me and I know that. But you don't know when to stop. You don't know when to quit and leave things alone. You don't know when to put something on the back burner and leave it be. You're as stubborn as a junkyard dog on fresh meat. It cost you your first wife, your job and almost your daughter, and made you a drunk. Janet's in Chicago and you're here alone because you just don't know when to fucking quit. What are you trying to do, drive everybody away who loves you? Because that's what it seems like. There, I said my piece."

The entire time Walt was talking I could feel Jane's glare on me.

Then I snapped.

I was up and over the new card table in one bound and landed on Walt's chest. The impact knocked Walt's chair backward to the sand and I came down hard on his stomach with my right fist cocked.

"Oh, fuck," Jane said and hit me flush in the face with pepper spray.

I covered my eyes and rolled off Walt to the sand.

"All right, all right, it's just some pepper spray," Jane said as she knelt beside me.

My eyes burned like fire and I could barely breathe, but I forced my hands away from my eyes and tried to stand. "You . . . fuck . . . ing," I snarled at Walt in between gasps.

Jane sat on my back. "Come on, Bekker, I don't want to hit you up again," she said. "This shit comes out of my budget."

I relaxed and let my chest touch the sand.

Walt stood up and dusted sand off his pants.

"I put you in for reinstatement," Walt said. "When you go before the board and they ask you what I just did, what are you gonna do, asshole? 'Cause if you go Mel Gibson on them like you did me, you'll never wear a badge again."

I forced my eyes open for a moment.

Walt picked up the Pat's box from the card table, turned and walked to his car. I heard the engine start and then he drove away.

I snapped my eyes closed. The burning was just too much.

"I'm getting up now, Bekker," Jane said. "Just relax."

She stood up and I heard her go into the trailer. I rolled and sat up, but my eyes burned so badly I still couldn't open them.

I heard Jane return and set something on the card table. "Give me your hand," she said.

I held out my right hand. Jane took it, tugged me to my feet and guided me to my chair. "Now just sit down and shut the fuck up for once in your stupid life," she said. I heard her do something and then felt a cold washcloth was wiping my eyes.

"Walt's right, you know," Jane said.

She dipped the washcloth into the pan of cold water on the table and continued to dab and wipe at my eyes until things quieted down and I could open them.

"Do I get a lollipop now?" I said.

Jane took her seat and grabbed her pack of smokes. "You'll never have a better friend than Walt."

"I know."

"And he is right."

"You said that already."

"So what are you going to do?"

"You maced me and sat on me," I said.

"I should have let you punch Walt's head in?"

"Don't you have a department to run?"

"I'm running it from right here," Jane said. "So what are you going to do?"

"About Walt or Amanda Felton?"

"If it makes you happy, both."

"First I'm going to take a shower and wash this shit off me, then I'll go see Walt," I said. "After that I'll let you know what I'm gonna do next."

Jane stood up. "Remember we're partners on this."

"I haven't forgotten," I said.

Jane turned to the card table. "Goddammit, he took the donuts."

TWENTY-FOUR

After twenty minutes in a hot shower I felt human again. I dressed quickly in one of the spiffy warm-up suits Janet picked out for me last year, teal in color, and put black walking shoes on my feet.

Outside my trailer, I plopped down in my chair with a fresh mug of coffee and thought about the apology I owed Walt.

It's easy to apologize to a stranger. It's not so easy when it's your best friend of thirty years and former partner. I was mentally composing the words when another tiny piece of the puzzle fell into my lap.

My cell phone rang. On the other end of the call was Robert Felton.

"Mr. Bekker?" Felton said.

"What can I do for you, Robert?"

"I've been thinking long and hard about what you said, about remembering something that might be important."

"And?"

"I didn't remember . . . I mean, it was nothing at the time, but in thinking back it strikes me as a little odd."

"What strikes you as a little odd?"

"Oh, something that happened over the 4th of July weekend when I last visited . . . my brother and Amanda," Felton said. "I was having coffee in the kitchen. Norman was planning a big barbeque and ran downtown for some last-minute supplies. Amanda asked me if she could borrow my cell phone. I didn't think anything of it at the time, but there are three phones in the house, including one in her room. What do you think it means?"

"What's your cell phone number?" I said. "I'd like to check it out."

Felton gave me the number and I scribbled it on the notepad on the card table. "Did you make any calls yourself that day?"

"Three or four to my dealership," Felton said. "I had a weekend sale going on. Do you think it means something?"

"Everything means something, Mr. Felton," I said.

I walked into Walt's office without knocking and said, "Over the 4th of July weekend, Amanda Felton borrowed her uncle's cell phone and made some calls. I want to have the numbers traced and see who she talked to."

From behind his desk, Walt looked at me. "Is that your apology?"

I sighed and dropped into a chair opposite the desk. "You're gonna make me say it?"

"Sorry, but I don't do Braille," Walt said.

"I lost my temper not at what you said but because what you said is true," I said. "And I wouldn't have hit you, you know that. I just snapped for a second is all, more mad at me than you."

Walt grinned. "Jane got you good, didn't she?"

"My eyes still burn," I said.

"You know I didn't mean one word of that bullshit," Walt said. "But if you think I sideswiped you, wait until the review board goes after you."

"How many?"

"Nine. Can't be less than a seven to two vote."

"My chances?"

"I don't know," Walt said. "I put my two cents in, wrote a

glowing disposition and got a few endorsements from the state and local justice departments. The rest is up to you, old friend."

I nodded.

"Want some coffee?"

I nodded again.

Walt picked up his phone and ordered coffee from the deli across the street. By the time he hung up, I was puffing on the e-cigarette.

"And what is with that stupid thing?" Walt said.

"My daughter is weaning me," I said.

Walt stared at me.

"So are you going to give Venus the cell number or not?" I said.

"This will cost you lunch," Walt said.

Walt drove us to the upscale restaurant located in the Bay Harbor Hotel, where the county elite moor their speedboats and yachts and other such water toys. There was a forty-five minute wait for a table.

Walt flashed his captain's badge and a window table for two magically appeared. We had a great view of a dozen or more jet skis moored along the very long dock.

"Look at that blue one," Walt said. "Eighteen grand. I priced one at the beginning of the summer."

"What for? You don't even like the water."

"Elizabeth is nagging me to start thinking about retirement and wanting a summer home and all that crap," Walt said. "I'm just thinking ahead."

"Plenty of room on the beach for another trailer," I said.

"Yeah, sell that one to Elizabeth," Walt sneered.

Lunch cost me one hundred and thirty-five dollars. I had a steak so tender I could have cut it with a fork. Walt had a chicken/steak combo. We both had cheesecake and coffee for dessert.

On our second cups of coffee, Walt got the call from Venus at the station. He pulled out his notepad and pen and scribbled on a page while he held his cell phone to his ear.

"Well?" I said when he hung up.

"Felton made four calls to his dealership," Walt said.

"He told me that," I said.

"And one call was made to a private cell phone belonging to James Crawford," Walt said.

"Anybody else?" I said.

"No. So who's James Crawford?"

"Amanda babysat for the Crawford family on the island," I said.

Walt nodded. "She was probably calling about a job."

"Most likely," I said.

"But you're going to check it out anyway?"

"Yeah."

I paid for lunch and we took a walk along the dock while I lit up an e-cigarette.

"Eighteen grand," Walt said as he looked at a blue jet ski for two.

"Is there anybody I know on the review board?" I said.

Walt shook his head. "All appointed by a state committee. They review for every police agency in the state. The hearing will take place at the capitol in a state building. And three visits to a shrink are also mandatory."

"Marvelous," I said.

TWENTY-FIVE

I waited at the car entrance ramp to the ferry on the mainland side for about an hour before Michael Crawford showed up in his blue sedan.

He didn't see me.

An attendant removed the barrier to the entrance ramp at six-thirty p.m. I drove my car slowly behind Crawford's. A total of ten cars boarded.

I didn't get out of my car until we were well under way. I stood at a railing and watched Crawford, who was still in his car and talking on a cell phone. I waited until he was off the phone to approach his car and tap lightly on his window.

Crawford looked at me for a moment. Then the lights came on in his eyes and he lowered the window. "Bekker, right?" he said.

"How are you, Mr. Crawford?"

"Good," Crawford said. "So what brings you back to the island?"

"Actually, I was on my way to speak to your son," I said.

"James? What for?"

"James is eighteen now, so I'll wait and ask him directly," I said. "Is he at home?"

"I'm his father," Crawford said. "I have a right to know."

"No, you don't," I said. "But if James allows it, you're welcome to sit in on the conversation. I'll ask him."

I turned and walked back to the railing. Behind me I heard

Crawford slam his car door. Then his hand was on my right arm.

"Remove your hand, please," I said.

There was a slight hesitation.

"I wasn't asking," I said.

Crawford lowered his hand. "Sorry, but I'm a bit upset here."

"Understandable," I said. "However, James is now an adult and what I have to ask him is privileged, and he may not want you to hear it. So why don't we wait and ask him if he wants you to sit in or not."

"What if I refuse to let you in my house?" Crawford said.

"You don't own the street," I said.

"All right, Bekker, we'll wait," Crawford said.

I waited on the street for thirty-seven minutes for James to return from his late afternoon run. I spotted him before he saw me and I waved to him from a distance of about fifty yards. He slowed his pace to a jog and finally a walk.

"You're that private investigator guy from a few weeks ago," he said when he were within earshot. "I forgot your name."

"John Bekker," I said.

"Yeah, I remember now," James said. "What are you doing here?"

"Came to see you."

"I mean in the street."

Up close, shirtless, James Crawford was a wall of muscle, heavier than I remembered from my last visit.

"I pegged you at two twenty-five, but you're a bit more than that," I said.

"Two thirty-eight," James said. "You came back here to ask my weight?"

"About Amanda Felton."

"I already told you what I know," James said. "Which is nothing."

"Something new came up that involves you," I said.

James looked at me.

I looked at him.

You can tell a great deal about a person, especially a young person, by their reaction to a surprise or a threat. In James's case, his eyes widened just a bit as his eyebrows formed arcs and his lips drew back in a nervous smile.

"I'm in the street because you're eighteen and your father doesn't have to know what I'm about to ask you," I said.

"I got nothing to hide from my dad," James said.

"Very well, let's go in the house."

James led us inside where Michael Crawford was in the living room, seated on the sofa with a newspaper. I knew by his shadow behind the pulled drapes at the living room window that he'd been watching us in the street only moments ago.

Crawford tossed the newspaper on the coffee table. "My son has no secrets from me," he said.

"That's right," James said.

"Okay, then," I said. "On the 4th of July weekend Amanda Felton called you on your cell phone, James. Why?"

"What are you . . . she never called me on my cell phone," James said.

"Cell phone numbers can be traced just like hard line phones, James," I said.

"I don't know what you're talking about."

"I do," Michael Crawford said.

James and I looked at Crawford as he stood up from the sofa.

"You went out to do your roadwork," Crawford said. "I was in the kitchen on the phone with some people from work. You left your phone on the table. After I hung up your phone rang and I answered it. It was Amanda. She wanted to know if we still needed her for the following weekend. I told her yes."

"How did she get your cell number, James?" I said.

"I gave her my cell, home and James's cell as emergency contacts," Crawford said. "My guess is she tried the house phone first and when it was busy she went down to the next number."

"And you didn't know about that?" I said to James.

He shook his head.

"It slipped my mind," Crawford said. "She was our babysitter, for God's sake. Is there anything else?"

"What size shoe do you wear, Mr. Crawford?" I said.

"What the fuck does that have to do with anything?" Crawford said.

"A great deal," I said.

"Twelve," Crawford said.

"James?" I said.

"Fourteen," James said.

"Happy now?" Crawford said.

"For the moment," I said.

"Goodbye then," Crawford said. "And if you feel the need to ask any more questions, direct them to my attorney."

I looked at Crawford. "Let's hope it doesn't come down to where you need an attorney."

I stood against the railing of the ferry with the e-cigarette and my cell phone. I'd tweaked and got a reaction. I fired round one and held the second bullet in reserve.

"Walt, can you dig up everything there is to know about Michael Crawford?" I said.

"Everything?" Walt said.

"Pretty much."

"Because?"

"He's a liar."

TWENTY-SIX

Sometimes when the best course of action is to simply just think I take a chair down to the beach and watch the waves crest and break. The repetition of the waves rolling in and out over and over again has a calming, almost soothing effect and if nothing else helps to clear the mind.

Hawaii was a distant memory even though I'd been home only a few weeks.

Norman Felton, a man who never hurt anybody until he beat a kid into a coma with a baseball bat, died from a gunshot wound and would never be able to explain his motives or defend his actions.

A lost earring.

Blood spatter on the rug.

A missing girl.

Janet was still very much angry with me. I knew that because she didn't call me. She asked for space and I gave it to her because I owed her that much. She was too strong-willed and determined a person to do something when her mind was made up not to, so I would have to ride out the full thirty days' banishment to the dog house.

Meanwhile, I had a different problem to solve.

A kid in a coma who in all likelihood was just an innocent victim in the wrong place at the wrong time.

Michael Crawford, father of James Crawford, a man protecting his son.

From what?

Michael Crawford was willing to lie. What else was he willing to do?

James Crawford, high-school star quarterback and soon to be college star on a full Monty scholarship.

Amanda Felton. *Where are you? If you're still alive why haven't you come forward? If you're dead, who murdered you? And why?*

As a cop you're taught to ignore emotion and follow the evidence.

A seemingly docile man drives to the high school in such a rage he beats a kid with a baseball bat, ignores the deputies called to the scene, and pays for that with his life.

Ubaldo Montero, a kid from another country on the student exchange program who volunteered to work on field detail for extra credit and probably never even heard of the Feltons.

The soup of thoughts cooking inside my head was bubbling over. Follow the liar and find out why he lied.

"Dad, what are you doing?" Regan said from behind me.

"Thinking," I said.

"Clayton called a few minutes ago," Regan said. "He has to go away on business for the weekend. Something about surveying the stress of a bridge. He asked if we could watch Mark from Friday to Sunday."

"What did you tell him?"

"That you would call him back."

"Okay."

"Okay that he can stay with us, or okay you'll call him back?"

"Both."

"I brought your phone."

"Thanks."

"I'm going driving with Oz," Regan said. "My road test is next week."

"Wait a second," I said.

"What?"

"Just stand there in front of me for a second."

"What are you . . . ?"

"Right there."

Dressed in blue jeans, a white tee shirt, baseball cap and white jogging shoes, Regan was a tiny bird with bright feathers. There is a feeling that hits a father in the gut like a Marciano punch when he looks at his daughter and realizes just how much he loves her.

What would a man do to protect his tiny bird?

I already knew the answer to that question. Not so long ago when a hit man put his hands on Regan I broke his fucking neck.

Norman Felton was protecting his tiny bird.

From what?

"Dad, are you okay?" Regan said.

"Yeah," I said. "Go ahead with Oz and I'll call Clayton."

Regan kissed me on the cheek. "Don't sit here too long," she said. "The tide's coming in and you'll get waterlogged."

After Regan left, I scanned saved numbers and hit the number for Clayton, Janet's ex-husband. On the third ring, Clayton picked up.

"Clayton, John Bekker," I said.

"Glad you called," Clayton said.

"Regan told me you have a business trip. What time do you need me to pick up Mark?"

"You're sure?"

"Yes."

"Four okay? My flight is at six."

"I'll be there."

"Thanks."

I hung up and watched the ocean for a bit more. My phone rang and I checked the number. It was Walt.

"Interesting man, Michael Crawford," Walt said.

We were at the new patio table. It was well after dark and the floodlights were on.

"How so?" I said.

Oz came out of my trailer and set a full pot of coffee on the table. There were already three mugs and a small pitcher of cream. He poured and sat.

"Crawford was all-state everything at State U until he blew out a knee in his senior year," Walt said. "Ran track, played some baseball, but as quarterback he was the star. Had pro scouts drooling over him until the knee went."

"He looks like he keeps himself in pretty good shape," I said. "What does he do for work?"

"After the pro career went south, he stayed in college and got a degree in business," Walt said. "Went to work as a rep for a large sporting goods manufacturer. He's now a regional manager overseeing sales and distribution. Has an office in town and is on the road ten days out of every thirty. Never misses his son's games, though. Not one in four years."

"What kind of money does he make?" I said.

"Around one hundred and fifty grand according to last year's tax returns."

"His wife died," I said. "Any girlfriends, women?"

"How the hell would I know that?" Walt said.

"Arrests, tickets, anything?" I said.

"Three years ago he got a speeding ticket in Vermont," Walt said. "Going seventy-four in a sixty-five."

"Gambling debts, owe money to anybody, hidden drug use . . . does he like young boys?" I said.

"Nothing," Walt said. "In fact, he has quite a tidy nest egg."

"This your suspect?" Oz said.

"Person of interest," I said.

"Person of interest, then," Oz said.

I took a sip from my mug and pulled out my electronic cigarette.

"What size shoe does he wear?" Walt said.

"Twelve," I said as I lit up.

"His son?"

"Fourteen."

"Doesn't fit size thirteen?" Oz said.

"No."

The door opened and Regan stepped out wearing a dark blue bathrobe. "You guys want some ice cream before I turn in?" she said.

"Only if I can get a hug and kiss goodnight," Walt said.

Regan gave all three of us hugs and kisses, then went back into the kitchen and returned with three bowls of chocolate ice cream topped with chocolate syrup and a dab of whipped cream.

"Make sure he doesn't puff on that e-cigarette too much," Regan said to Oz.

"How I do that?" Oz said. "The man can pick up a car."

"Yeah, but he's dumb as an ox," Regan said with a wink.

Spooning ice cream into his mouth, Walt let out a soft laugh. "The kid knows her father," he said.

Regan went inside and slid the door closed.

"Man, I've gained five pounds since you been back," Oz said to me.

"Then you can go running with me tomorrow," I said.

"I don't panic or do something that stupid until I put on another ten," Oz said and licked whipped cream off his spoon. "And then I only think about it."

"I have the same feelings about it myself," Walt said. He looked at me. "So what are you going to do?"

"Proceed," I said.

"That's no answer," Walt said. "And while you're proceeding, what about Jane?"

"I'll keep Jane in the dark for a while," I said. "If things blow up in my face at least she'll be clear of it."

"Clear of what?" Oz said.

"The process," I said.

"Man, I'm going to bed," Oz said. "Your process has given me a headache."

"I think that's ice cream brain freeze," I said.

"More like Bekker brain freeze," Oz said and carried his empty bowl into the trailer.

I finished my last bit of ice cream and washed down the sweetness with some coffee. "Keep digging, Walt," I said. "Maybe Mr. Perfect isn't so perfect."

"And maybe he's telling the truth about the girl calling about a babysitting job?" Walt said. "She was, after all, his babysitter."

"No," I said.

"You're sure?"

"Yes."

"How? You weren't there and the girl can't speak for herself at the moment."

"She waited until her father went into town for some barbeque supplies, and then asked her uncle to use his cell phone," I said. "Why? She had her own phone in her room. No, she didn't want anybody to know about the call she was making so she used a cell phone figuring it would be safe. I think she had something going with the Crawford boy and he gave her the earrings because people notice a ring, but junk jewelry is invisible."

Walt mulled that over. I sucked on the e-cigarette.

"Okay, it's possible," Walt admitted.

"More than possible," I said.

"Okay, it's probable, but that doesn't make what's-his-name Michael Crawford guilty of anything other than answering his son's phone," Walt said.

"Except that he lied," I said.

"And you're sure about that?"

"Positive."

Walt sighed, took a sip of coffee and said, "Want to talk about your hearing?"

"No."

"Janet?"

"No."

"You'll let me know what you're doing in case I have to bail you out."

"No."

"This is no way to get back in the good graces of the review board, Jack," Walt said.

"What is?" I said.

"Good point."

"Go home, Walt," I said. "I need some sleep."

Walt nodded. "I'll see what else I can dig up on Crawford." He stood up and walked to his sedan. "Jack?"

"Yeah?"

"Don't do anything to fuck up your review with the board."

"I'll do my best," I said.

"Yeah," Walt said. "That's what concerns me."

TWENTY-SEVEN

I sat in the stands with a crowd of two thousand and watched Regional High School take on a team from the western part of the state, the Bobcats. Regional was led by James Crawford and the Cats never stood a chance.

In the first quarter, James threw for two touchdowns and rushed up the middle for a third on second and five. The kid was a monster on the field.

His father was worse than any Little League dad I've ever seen.

In the first row behind Regional's bench, Michael Crawford screamed his head off on every play his son was involved in. He shouted advice before every pass or run, screamed at his son on an incompletion or a failed rush attempt, yelled at the coach and refs, and made an all-around complete fool of himself.

By halftime the score was Regional forty-two, Bobcats seven. Michael Crawford made his way down to the field before the coach entered the school locker room and the two exchanged heated words. I think the argument started when Crawford tried to enter the locker room with the team and the coach wouldn't allow it.

Reluctantly, Crawford returned to his seat.

I killed the twenty minutes of halftime by scanning the crowd and picking out the college scouts. It wasn't difficult to spot them. They all had clipboards and binders and made one call after another on cell phones.

The third quarter was a let-down period for James. He had seven incomplete passes, one fumble and only threw one touchdown pass. The Bobcats changed their game plan during halftime and they blitzed James for the entire period.

Michael Crawford all but went nuts on the sidelines. He was so bad the coach had to send school security to quiet him down.

Between periods, the coach made adjustments, and during the fourth period James threw for two touchdowns and rushed for a third. The final score was Regional seventy, Bobcats fourteen. James Crawford accounted for all seventy points via the pass or rushing, not counting the point after kicks. After the game, Michael Crawford rushed the field to hug James and caused a scene out of a bad sports movie.

I waited for the stands to empty and followed Michael Crawford to his car. I figured he had an hour's wait for James. I took advantage of that time and strolled across the parking lot to where Michael Crawford was leaning against his car, talking on his cell phone. He spotted me and quickly put the phone away.

"Bekker," he said. "What are you doing here?"

"Came to see the game," I said. "Or more specifically, to see your son play."

"And what did you see?"

"He's a giant among boys, but the monsters in the college lines will eat him alive," I said.

"What the fuck are you talking about?" Michael said. "All right, he had a bad third quarter, but he made fools of them in the fourth. That's what the great ones do, make adjustments."

"No wonder James secretly wants to play baseball," I said.

Michael Crawford went red in the face. "I'm done talking to you, Bekker. Get fucking lost."

"That's a fine attitude to take when here I came all this way just to return this to your son," I said and dipped my right hand into my pocket for Amanda's earring. I held my hand out palm up to show the jewelry to Crawford.

"What's that?" he said.

"Amanda Felton's missing earring," I said. "This is what you were looking for that day we surprised you at the Felton home. You remember, you hopped the fence, hit the sheriff in the head with a log."

Michael Crawford stared at the earring. His face went beet red again from anger. His hands balled into fists.

"Mr. Crawford, raise a hand to me and I promise you a quick trip to the dentist to replace your teeth," I said.

He unclenched his fists. Slowly, his gaze rose to meet mine. "I don't know what you're talking about," he said.

"Sure you do," I said. "Here, take it." I held the earring out to him. "It's what you were looking for, isn't it?"

"You're fucking crazy," Crawford said.

"Your son gave the earrings to her," I said. "I have proof of that. It won't take me long to put two and two . . ."

Crawford tried to sucker-punch me with a quick right hand. I sidestepped the punch, grabbed his arm and swung him face first into the hood of his car. He tried to struggle, but I pressed my arm against the back of his neck and pinned him down.

"Get the fuck off me!" Crawford shouted.

I released my arm from his neck and spun him around. We stood nose to nose.

"Mr. Crawford, I'm in an ugly place right now," I said. "Sometimes the only way to catch ugly is, you've got to become it. If you want a rematch I'd be happy to send you to the hospital. If you want to confess I'd be happy to listen."

"Confess?" Crawford said. "Confess to what?"

"Where is Amanda Felton?" I said.

"How the fuck should I know?"

"I ask again, where is Amanda Felton?"

"My attorney will deal with this," Crawford said.

"Fuck your attorney."

"There are laws to—"

"Fuck the laws," I said. "And fuck you, too."

Crawford stared at me. "I'll file a harassment complaint."

"Be my guest," I said. "That won't stop me and then everyone will know you have something to hide. That will catch the attention of a state prosecutor and they will send an investigator from the state police to see you. See you around, Mr. Crawford."

I left him speechless as I turned and walked to my car.

Second bullet fired.

Target hit.

Even if the bullet was a tad illegal.

If the review board could see me now.

Twenty-Eight

Clayton answered the front door to his condo dressed in a sports coat and tan khakis, white shirt and no tie. He looked at me. I looked at him.

"What?" I said.

"I appreciate this, Bekker," he said. "Mark will be right down."

"Clayton, would you relax," I said.

"Sorry," Clayton said. "You make me nervous."

"I came here at your request, not to hit you," I said.

A year ago, I came to talk to Clayton when a case I was working on got out of hand and I wanted to put Mark in protective custody. He acted like a jerk and I tagged him one in the stomach to un-jerk him. Since then he's been a nervous wreck when I'm around.

"I know," he said. "I'm acting like an idiot and I'm sorry."

"Uncle Jack," Mark said as he brushed past Clayton.

"All packed?" I said.

"And ready to go," Mark said.

"I'll bring him by Sunday night," I said to Clayton.

"Thanks again, Bekker," Clayton said.

I extended my right hand. Clayton looked at it and then extended his.

Regan and Mark looked for shells along the shoreline. It was low tide on a beautiful fall morning, warm enough to swim, bright enough to catch a tan.

I sat in my new lawn chair outside my trailer and watched Mark chase gulls while Regan picked at shells.

Oz occupied his chair next to mine. We each had mugs of coffee. I puffed on the e-cigarette and let the sun warm my face.

"Gonna fire up the grill?" Oz said. "It's almost noon."

I went to the grill and loaded in some new coals, squirted on some lighter fluid and tossed in a lit match. The coals burst into flames that spread quickly and I returned to my chair. "Michael Crawford is lying to protect his son," I said.

"You go to school to figure out a man would lie to protect his son?" Oz said.

I sucked in some smoke from the e-cigarette and blew out a ring of vapor.

"What would you do to protect Regan?" Oz said. "How far would you go?"

I looked down to the beach where Regan was splashing Mark by kicking up water.

"No need to answer that," Oz said. "We both know."

I got up to check the coals. The flames were out and the coals were graying nicely.

I spun around and looked at Oz. "I got nothing," I said. "Empty threats and flimsy evidence at best. You finished all my notes?"

Oz looked at the notepad on the card table.

"Give me a summation," I said and plopped into my seat.

"What, I'm Perry Mason now?" Oz said.

I looked at him.

"Okay, all right, jeez," Oz said. He picked up the notepad and flipped to the first page. "You want the long or short version?"

"Short," I said.

"Mr. Norman Felton drives from Midnight Island to the high school with a hundred percent mad on," Oz said. "He fights with an exchange student named Ubaldo Montero and beats the kid half to death with a baseball bat. Jane brings your ass into the mix because she's in over her head on detective work. Thanks to a busted window we now know the Montero boy was shagging fly balls with an unknown witness who we now think Norman Felton got confused over in his pissed-off state of mind and attacked the wrong kid. How am I doing so far?"

"Good."

"You and Jane play Nick and Nora and find blood and a missing earring on the floor, and somehow you figure out the girl has a cheap pair that look like the real thing and the Crawford boy may or may not have bought them for her at the mall. You go Mel Gibson on Mr. Michael Crawford and figure the man is protecting his son 'cause last 4th of July the girl borrowed her uncle's cell phone to call Mr. Crawford, possibly about a babysitting job as she is the man's babysitter. How's them coals?"

I went and took a peek. "About ten minutes," I said and returned to my chair.

"That's it," Oz said.

"What don't I have?" I said as I sucked on the e-cigarette.

"Clean lungs," Oz said. "And no real evidence any prosecutor could use in court."

"And?"

"No girl, no ransom note, and no evidence she was kidnapped or murdered."

"In other words, not a whole lot," I said.

"In other words, you got squat," Oz said.

"I'm going to have to squeeze Crawford and his son," I said. "I'll have to break them and get them to talk. It's the only way to get them to tell the truth."

"Legally or otherwise?" Oz said.

"If Jane didn't want otherwise she never would have brought me in," I said. "She knows that and so do I."

"That *otherwise* could put your ass in the jackpot," Oz said. "And screw up that review board hearing you got in . . . what is it, twenty-seven days?"

I went and tossed some burgers and dogs on the grill.

"A man is dead and his daughter is missing and it would be a miracle if she was still alive, but she probably isn't, and another kid is in a coma," I said. "Somebody has to answer for all that."

"Somebody?" Oz said.

"How do you want your burger?" I said.

After dark I sat in my chair and listened to the ocean.

I'd crossed the line with Michael Crawford. I knew that and so did he. I didn't care. The man was hiding something, protecting somebody, probably his son, and if he wasn't willing to give the information up I would have to take it from him.

The problem with visiting that ugly place is, it's easy to get used to being there. Cops who care too much, if there is such a thing, visit and find they have moved in and ugly becomes a permanent address.

Become a criminal to catch a criminal. It's not what the judicial system is supposed to be about, but when criminals walk free on technicalities and repeat their offenses, it becomes easy to cross that line to put them away.

Easy to cross over, difficult to cross back.

Oz was right, of course. I had a great deal to lose in my life right now and I knew it. Janet, for one thing. Regan was healthier and her future looked brighter than I ever could have imagined a year ago. And after more than a dozen years away from the job I had the opportunity to be a cop again.

All I had to do was do the right thing and not screw up.

That's what I told myself in Hawaii and look how well that turned out.

TWENTY-NINE

I played long ball toss on the beach with Mark. He wanted to practice his curveball and changeup, so I counted off sixty feet and played catcher while he got in some fairly good pitches.

Regan and Oz spent the afternoon practicing for Regan's driving test next week. Before any of us realized it the Sunday afternoon was gone and I needed to drive Mark back to Clayton's. I took the Marquis as Regan and Oz were still off somewhere practicing for the road test.

Halfway to Clayton's condo, Mark turned to look out his window and grew quiet and unusually sullen.

"Mark, is something wrong?" I said.

"No," Mark said and started to cry softly into the window.

Fifteen-year-old boys, even the sensitive types, just don't cry in public without a very good reason.

"Mark, what is it?" I said.

"Can we . . . can we stop somewhere for a few minutes?" Mark said.

"Sure."

A mile up the road I stopped at an ice cream stand that sold coffee. I ordered two dishes of chocolate ice cream and a coffee for me and we took seats at a vacant picnic table in the shade.

"So," I said as I spooned some ice cream into my mouth. "What's got you so upset?"

Mark ate some ice cream, cleared his throat and looked at me.

"I wasn't supposed to hear this and I didn't on purpose," he said.

I ate another spoonful. "Wasn't supposed to hear what on purpose?"

"Mom lied to me," Mark said. "And so did my dad."

"Did you think adults didn't lie?" I said. "If they didn't, I'd be out of a job."

"This is different," Mark said.

"How so?"

Mark licked his spoon and then sighed. "Maybe I shouldn't say any more."

"That's up to you," I said. "But just so you know, I'm always here for you and you can tell me anything."

Mark looked at me. "Even if it makes you mad?"

"When you get a little older you're going to find there are a lot of things that are difficult to say to people," I said. "If it's hurtful, try to find a way to say it so it lessens the blow. If it's something they need to know and might harm them, try to find a way to let them down gently. Understand?"

"Yes."

"Good."

"What about if it's something you're not supposed to know about and might hurt somebody; should you tell or keep quiet?"

"That depends on the who and the what," I said. "And if it's important enough or not to hurt or spare someone's feelings."

"You're not making this easy."

"Being an adult isn't easy," I said. "And you'll find that out more and more as you go along."

Mark ate some ice cream, licked the spoon and nodded. "When you were in Hawaii, Mom was very upset about that," he said.

"I know."

"When you didn't come home, Dad started coming around more and more," Mark said. "He even stayed over in the guest room a few times. Then they went out on a date to dinner and a movie like they were still married."

I nodded and waited for more. "They're adults and were married for a long time. That's not exactly a lie for them to . . ."

"I don't mean that part," Mark said. "I heard them talking about three weeks ago when they came back from the movies and thought I was asleep. Dad told Mom he could visit her in Chicago for a weekend to . . . he said to evaluate their situation and she said yes. I think they might be getting back together, Uncle Jack." He looked at me with mist in his eyes.

"You know, usually when a kid's parents are divorced and there is a chance they might get back together again, the kid is a lot happier than you are about it," I said.

"Honestly?"

"Yes."

"I like them better divorced."

"Divorced or married, they're still your parents," I said.

"Divorced, they don't fight and yell at each other," Mark said. "Married, all they did was fight."

"Then," I said. "People change."

"You sound like you don't care."

"I care a great deal," I said. "Because I love your mom and wanted to marry her and still do."

"It sounds like there should be a *but* in there," Mark said.

I ate a bit more ice cream, set aside the bowl and sipped some coffee.

"In a sense I screwed up," I said. "I can never repay her for all the help she has given me the past two years when I sobered up, and a long time ago after her sister was killed. When I was trying to understand what happened in Hawaii and I stayed for six weeks, your mom wanted to come there and help me get through it. I told her I needed to be alone to work things out. I think she felt I was shutting her out and I'm sure that hurt her a great deal."

"You didn't do it on purpose," Mark said.

"No, I didn't, but I'm sure it hurt her just as much as if I had," I said.

"Okay, so you hurt her feelings," Mark said. "I get that, I think. What I don't get is how come they're getting back together."

"That I can't answer," I said. "If I were to guess, I would say it has a lot to do with my shortcomings. Your mom is at the age where stability is important in a relationship. Being able to count on someone always being there for you and you for them is an important quality in a happy relationship."

"And she doesn't get that from you?"

"I don't think so, especially after Hawaii."

"But didn't Mom ask you to do that?" Mark said. "Check out her boss or whatever that was."

"Yes," I said. "But to be honest, I couldn't wait for something to do that would occupy my time besides looking for a nine-to-five job, television and washing dishes. So when she asked me to do her a favor I jumped at the chance. I think your mom probably feels that I'll never be able to give her what she wants in a relationship because I'll always be looking over my shoulder for the next bad guy I should be after, instead of doing laundry and making beds."

"Washing dishes sucks," Mark said.

I had to laugh. "Yes, it does."

"So what do we do now?"

"You do nothing and keep this to yourself for now," I said. "I'll do the same until your mom gets back and then we'll talk."

Mark nodded as he ate a spoonful of ice cream. "Whatever

happens I don't lose you, right?" he said.

"I may not wind up as your stepdad, but I'll always be your uncle," I said. "And nothing can change that. Come on, let's finish our ice cream and I'll drive you home."

"Dad, I'm going with Oz to practice night driving," Regan said. "Want to come along?"

"Go ahead, hon," I said. "I have some work to do."

Regan kissed me on the cheek. "Won't be more than an hour," she said.

I watched as Regan entered her Impala and drove down the beach to Oz's trailer where he was waiting for her. He got in and she drove off the beach and out of sight.

I built a bonfire and brewed a pot of coffee. I sat and drank a mug and sucked on the e-cigarette.

What Mark told me earlier didn't come as a total shock to my system. Even though they were divorced for years when I came on to the scene, Clayton never fell out of love with Janet and he made that no secret. And it isn't all that unusual for divorced couples to find themselves getting back together after a decade or more when they've realized that whatever their differences were, they no longer existed or mattered, and the two of them fit each other like an old shoe lost in the closet.

My cell phone was on the new patio table beside the mug of coffee. I hadn't looked at it all day. I picked it up and checked messages. There were a dozen or more. From Jane, Walt, Paul Lawrence and Joey.

I stared at the phone for a moment. Each message also gave the number of times the person called.

"Of course," I said aloud when a light bulb in my head came on.

I called Jane.

"Bekker, I called you . . ." she said.

"I know," I said. "Are you in the office?"

"Yes."

"Stay there."

I hung up and called Walt.

Walt said, "Jack, the meeting with the review board has been rescheduled for . . ."

"Are you in the office?"

"Home."

"Stay there."

I hung up and called Paul Lawrence.

Lawrence said, "Jack, nothing on the . . ."

"Do you know how to do a conference call?" I said.

"Yes."

"Good."

Fifteen minutes later, Paul Lawrence said, "Jack, Walt, Jane, everybody on?"

"Yes," I said.

"Also," Jane said.

"Make it three," Walt said.

"Jane, do you still have the phone records from the Felton home?" I said.

"Yes."

"For the month that she disappeared?"

"Again, yes. Why?"

"What are you aiming at, Jack?" Walt said.

"We know Amanda called the Crawford kid on her uncle's cell phone," I said. "I don't believe for one minute it was about a babysitting job. Let's get the phone company to provide actual incoming numbers for June, July and August and see how many times the Crawford kid's cell number pops up."

"That could take a while, Jack," Jane said. "I need to see a judge and . . ."

"Paul doesn't," I said. "And to check James Crawford's cell calls in and out for, say, three months."

"I still need a reason," Lawrence said.

"You're looking for terrorists," I said.

"On Midnight Island?" Lawrence said.

"The terrorists who took down the World Trade Center stayed in Maine at a small inn by the mall," I said. "Why not Midnight Island?"

Lawrence sighed. "Give me twenty-four hours and I'll call you back on your cell phone."

"What are you looking for, Jack?" Walt said.

"I'm looking over my shoulder, Walt."

"What the hell does that . . . ?"

"Let's meet at my trailer about this same time," I said. "Okay to call back then, Paul?"

"Mr. Bekker . . . I mean, Jack," Joey said. "I called you earlier."

"I know. I was tied up for a while. How are you doing?"

"Sick as a sick dog can get," Joey said. "Nausea, mostly. I can't keep anything down except for dry crackers and shaved ice."

"That's to be expected," I said. "Did you ask the doctors?"

"They said I can have visitors as early as next week."

"Then you'll have some," I said.

"Mr. Bekker . . . I mean, Jack . . . I don't think I'm going to make it," Joey said.

"What do the doctors say?"

"They're very optimistic."

"But you're not?"

"No. The treatments are bad enough, but afterwards I feel so sick—like I can feel myself dying inside," Joey said.

"That's because you are," I said. "The treatments kill the cancer and in a sense a little part of you. Once the cancer starts to die I'm sure you'll feel a whole lot better."

"Ya think?"

"I do."

"So you'll come see me next week?"

"That is a promise."

"Don't forget you also promised me a surprise."

"I never forget a promise," I said.

I was working angles in my mind like a game of pool when Regan returned from her practice run with Oz.

"How did it go?" I said.

Regan took the chair next to me. "I only hit three garbage cans and the bumpers of two parked cars."

"Still can't see over the hood, huh?"

"Well, I didn't grow in the past two weeks," Regan said. "What am I going to do on the road test?"

"Use a smaller car," I said. "We'll rent a compact a few days before the test. You can practice with that and use it to take the test."

Regan wagged her finger at me. "I knew you were good for something."

"Feel like taking a trip to New York?" I said.

"To see that sick girl?"

I nodded.

"When?"

"Next week, maybe Monday. Oz can watch Molly for a few days."

"Absolutely."

"Good, because I promised her I'd bring her a surprise."

"What are you going to get her?"

"You."

"Me?"

"Well, you are a prize," I said.

THIRTY

Wasting time is not as easy or as pleasurable as it sounds.

Just ask any person who retired too early. There is only so much daytime television, digging in the garden, fishing for catches you will never eat and traveling to places you never really wanted to see in the first place. A hobby is just another way of killing excess time.

One of my hobbies is playing a mental game of connect the dots.

Dot A. Norman Felton takes his car across the ferry from Midnight Island to the high-school football field where he beats Ubaldo Montero into a coma with a baseball bat. Montero was more than likely hitting fly balls to a person unknown.

B. Jane's deputies are called to the scene by Sheryl Johnson, a teacher catching up on paperwork on a Saturday afternoon.

C. In an out-of-control rage, Felton turns the bat on the deputies and is accidently shot for his trouble. He later dies from a blood clot-related heart attack. Montero remains in a coma.

D. Amanda Felton, Norman Felton's fourteen-year-old daughter, is missing and could have been missing the day of the bat incident. Reasons unknown.

E. Amanda Felton babysat for neighbors on Midnight Island, including the Crawford family.

F. Amanda had over three hundred dollars in her piggy bank. If she ran away from home, why didn't she take the money?

G. On a return trip to the Felton home, an intruder was in the house, escaped through the back door and ran into the woods. He had a key? Why and how? Said intruder escaped the woods after hitting Jane on the head with a large branch. He wore a size thirteen boot. The vacuum cleaner had been moved from one closet to another.

H. A month earlier Amanda made a suspicious phone call using her uncle's cell phone. She called James Crawford, son of Michael Crawford. Michael Crawford claimed the call was about a babysitting job for his younger daughter. James is the star quarterback for the regional high school and drooled over by college scouts. Father wears a size twelve, son wears a fourteen.

I. Closer inspection of the Felton home produced some blood spatter and one diamond earring belonging to Amanda. It is believed that Felton gave the earrings to Amanda for her birthday. Did Felton strike Amanda on the day of the incident, knocking her to the floor and dislodging one earring? Was the intruder using the vacuum to try to find the missing earring?

J. Later discovered that Amanda had a pair of costume jewelry earrings that may have been purchased by James Crawford and given to her. Why?

K. Michael Crawford is a male soccer mom and protective of his son to the point of violence. Denies his son's involvement with Amanda Felton on any level other than James sometimes picked her up and dropped her off when she babysat his kid sister.

L. The dots don't add up.

Giving a kid a pair of earrings doesn't a crime make.

Norman Felton can't say why he beat the Montero kid because he died, but whoever broke into the Felton home most definitely knows why and that is most likely the reason he attacked Jane to avoid detection.

I needed more dots. I owed it to Amanda Felton, alive or dead.

There was that word again. Owed.

Did I really owe it to a young woman I'd never met to find

out who killed her a dozen years ago.

"Dad, what are you doing?" Regan said.

"Working."

"It looks a lot like sitting and staring into space."

"That, too."

"When I do the exact same thing Father Tomas puts me on a couch for forty-five minutes," Regan said.

"Want to go for a run?" I said.

"You want me to run with you?" Regan said. "I have tiny little legs."

"We'll take tiny little strides," I said.

"All right," Regan said. "Give me a minute to change."

"Good idea," I said. "Me, too."

Five minutes later we walked down to the ocean wearing shorts, tank tops and running shoes.

"Stretch first," I said and took Regan through ten minutes of limbering-up exercises.

"Now what?" Regan said.

"We run."

"Slowly, I hope."

I kept the pace to about an eleven-minute mile for the first half mile. To my left, Regan stayed with me. I gradually stepped it up a bit so she wouldn't notice the increase. At around a mile she started to suck wind.

"Breathe in through your nose and out through your mouth," I said.

"How about I puke through my mouth," Regan said between gasps.

"Just another half mile," I said.

"Another half . . ."

"In and out," I said. "In nose, out mouth."

"What, I'm the Karate Kid now?" Regan said. "When do I

learn how to punch?"

"First learn balance," I said.

"Funny, Dad."

"Keep going, we're almost there."

I guided us to a mile and a half mark and slowed us to a stop. Regan collapsed to the sand. I sat next to her.

"Dear God, why did you bless me with this hyperactive idiot for a father," Regan gasped.

"It wasn't that bad," I said.

"We're walking back, right?" Regan said.

"No."

Regan flopped onto her back and covered her eyes with her arms. Her earrings sparkled in the sun.

"I see you're wearing your earrings," I said.

"I decided never to take them off," Regan said. "That way I won't lose them."

"Because they're real diamonds?" I said.

"No, silly," Regan said. "Because you gave them to me."

"What if someone else gave them to you, say Walt or Oz?"

"They would still be valuable to me, but not as much."

"So you wouldn't wear them all the time, then?"

"Probably not. Why?"

"Just trying to understand the whole earring/woman thing."

"Good luck trying to figure out the woman/anything thing."

"You got that right," I said. "Are you ready for the return trip?"

"Can I call a cab?"

"No."

While Regan took a shower, I worked the heavy bag, cranked out sets of push-ups and pull-ups, and let my thoughts free-fall. Regan was showered and dressed by the time I called it quits.

"Walt and Jane are coming by tonight for a pow-wow," I said.

"Let's hit town for some burgers, dogs and whatnot."

"Sure, just as soon as you take a shower," Regan said. "Otherwise I'll have to walk you to town on a leash."

THIRTY-ONE

Grilled burgers, hot dogs, fries and a vat of baked beans eaten in front of a raging bonfire makes for a pleasant evening at the beach, made even more pleasant by the fact that none of us talked shop while we ate.

"Dad, Oz and I are going out for a practice run," Regan announced when we were on after-dinner coffee.

And then Jane smoked a cigarette and I sucked on a fake one and we waited for Paul Lawrence to call.

Finally, right around the time he said he would call, he did.

"I'm going to do a conference call like yesterday," Lawrence said. "Jack, hang up and I'll call one by one."

Fifteen minutes later we were all connected on our cell phones.

"The big news on the Felton hard line is there is none," Lawrence said. "If you're looking for a pattern or repeat calls, there are very few."

"Did you run down the numbers?" I said.

"No. I figure you'll do that," Lawrence said. "I'll email you the list of—"

"I don't have email," I said.

"Fax?" Lawrence said.

"Nope."

"You do know what century this is?"

"Send it to me," Jane said.

"What about the Crawford kid?" I said.

"He's a kid," Lawrence said. "Made about seven hundred calls on his cell phone in a three-month span. I'll email the list to Jane."

"Any repeat numbers?" I said.

"Shitloads," Lawrence said. "Have fun with it, you crazy kids."

"Paul, do the lists include who the recipient is?" I said.

"Just the number," Paul said. "That's how it works. We look for area codes and numbers called over and over again. If we see something suspicious, we run that number down to its origin. Like I said, have fun."

"Okay, thanks, Paul," I said.

"Good luck," Lawrence said. "And I really mean that."

After Lawrence hung up I went inside for a fresh pot of coffee and then filled our mugs.

"Probably a thousand numbers on the two lists," Walt said. "It's not my case but I'd like to help. When you get the lists we can use Venus to narrow down the repeat numbers and do a reverse search on them."

"Jane?" I said.

She nodded.

"Say ten o'clock at my office," Walt said. He stood up and walked to his car.

"Hey, if you see my kid bumping into cars or knocking over a stop sign, it's because she's short," I said.

"I'll pretend I know what that means," Walt said. He drove off the beach and out of sight.

"I gotta go, too," Jane said. Instead of standing, she lit another cigarette.

"Something on your mind besides a thousand phone calls?" I said.

"My husband moved in with Miss Wash and Dry," Jane said.

"Sorry to hear that," I said.

"Yeah."

"How old is he now?"

"Around the same as you."

"So when he's done with his middle-aged man trauma and comes begging to take him back?" I said.

"No," Jane said. "No way. I'm not the-forgive-and-forget type. What about you and Janet?"

"There is the strong possibility that while I was soul-searching in Hawaii her ex-husband Clayton side-stepped me," I said.

"Want me to arrange for him to have a hundred parking tickets issued to his car?" Jane said.

"Tempting, but no," I said.

Jane stood up and tossed the cigarette into the bonfire. "Oh the fucked up people some people marry," she said and walked to her cruiser.

"I'll see you around ten," I said.

I watched Jane's cruiser fade away into the dark and then added a few logs to the fire.

Molly was suddenly by my side and jumped onto my lap. She rubbed my hands with her head, telling me she wanted to be scratched. I obliged her by scratching her ears. She curled up into a ball and started to purr loudly.

"Looks like it's just you and me," I said as I continued to scratch. "Just like in the beginning."

THIRTY-TWO

Jane picked me up at nine-thirty and we stopped for egg sandwiches and coffee on the way to the police station.

I carried the paper bags full of breakfast, Jane carried a cardboard box full of reports and the phone records emailed to her by Paul Lawrence. We sat around Walt's desk to eat our sandwiches and pick through the evidence.

"Looks like eleven hundred calls placed over the three-month span," Jane said. "Almost eight hundred by the Crawford boy. What in the hell do these kids talk about, they're on the phone so much?"

"Girls," Walt said. "What did you think?"

"I think I need a smoke," Jane said.

"Not in here you . . ." Walt said as she lit up.

"Did you say something?" Jane said.

"This is my office," Walt said.

"I know," Jane said. "It says so on the door."

"Let's get started," I said.

We moved to Walt's conference table. Walt took several legal pads and pens and we took chairs side by side.

"This is going to take a while," I said. "Can we send out for a pot of coffee?"

"Good idea," Walt said.

"And an ashtray," Jane said.

Walt sighed. "What the hell," he said.

★ ★ ★ ★ ★

About an hour and several cups of coffee later, we had two lists completed of the Felton home number. Repeat calls to a dozen numbers outgoing. I recognized several grouped together at the end of June and early July as belonging to James Crawford. Incoming calls showed a grouping of calls from James Crawford's cell phone to the Felton home during the same time period.

All the calls were made during the afternoon between three-thirty and five-thirty. Before Norman Felton arrived home from work.

"No weekend calls to Crawford's cell," I said.

"My gut tells me those calls weren't about a babysitting job," Jane said.

"No," I said.

"Next list," Walt said.

"Hold on," I said. "Let's highlight any 800 or 877 numbers."

After we did that, we tackled James Crawford's monumental call log from his cell phone.

"For God's sake, couldn't Paul do this with the click of a button?" Jane said after thirty minutes of cross-referencing.

"They don't work that way," Walt said. "They look for suspicious area codes and repeat calls to and from those codes. Some guy in Cleveland calls Syria a dozen times in a week, they go in and look for chatter."

"Chatter?" Jane said. "Is that the official term?"

"What's this?" I said and ran my finger over a number James Crawford called seven times in one week just after the 4th of July.

Walt and Jane looked at the number. "We saw this one, I think," Walt said.

Jane grabbed the Felton hard-line log and ran a finger down the pages. "Yeah," she said when she found the number.

"Walt, put your phone on speaker," I said.

Walt went to his desk and put his phone on speaker. "What's that number?" he said.

Jane read it off and Walt punched in the digits. After two rings a pleasant-sounding female voice answered. "Family Planning Center," she said. "How may I help you?"

Walt, Jane and I exchanged glances.

"Sorry, wrong number," Walt said and disconnected.

Jane sat back in her chair and fired up a cigarette. "She had an abortion," she said, and blew smoke.

"Suddenly I feel like I could use some fresh air," Walt said.

"Let's grab some lunch," I said.

Walt drove us to the burger/seafood place along the public beach. We sat outside on the deck where a soft salt-sea breeze off the ocean cooled the otherwise hot day. A flock of gulls waited below the deck and squawked loudly for scraps.

"At least now we know what made Felton blow his stack," Walt said. "Somebody soiled his little girl."

"If by somebody you mean James Crawford, I agree with you," Jane said.

"We don't know that for sure," Walt said.

"Maybe not, but what do you think all those calls are?" Jane said. "And Family Planning was called from both numbers. He gave her earrings. She babysat for the family. A lot of alone time between two teenagers, it's not too difficult to imagine those teenage hormones getting carried away."

"Yeah, I know," Walt said. "Is that place city or county?"

"County," Jane said. "I know where it is."

"Jack, what do you think?" Walt said.

"I think I'll have a bacon burger," I said. "With fries."

★ ★ ★ ★ ★

I sucked on the e-cigarette as Jane drove me back to my trailer.

"Bekker, I think we should talk to Family Planning," Jane said.

"I know."

"And the Crawford boy again."

"I know."

"And ask a judge for a warrant to search the Crawford home."

"I know."

"Is that all you're going to say is 'I know'?" Jane said.

"What time you got?" I said.

"Four."

"Let's go see Family Planning," I said.

Jane nodded and stuck a cigarette between her lips. "Got a light?"

"Not anymore," I said and sucked on the e-cigarette.

THIRTY-THREE

"I'm sorry, Sheriff, but our policy is never to give out personal information," the chipper-looking woman at the reception desk in the lobby at Family Planning said.

"We're investigating a homicide and missing-persons case that is connected to your clinic," Jane said. "And we need your help."

"I'm sorry, but I just can't give you personal information," the woman said.

"I'll get a court order," Jane said.

"Do what you have to do," the woman said. "My responsibility is to our clients."

"Clients?" Jane said. "I'm talking about a fourteen-year-old girl here."

"The age of our clients doesn't matter," the woman said. "Our policy is—"

"Fuck your policy," Jane said. "And fuck you, too."

"Excuse me?" the woman said. "I don't think—"

"Yeah, I can tell," Jane said. "So let me think for you. I'll get a court order from a judge and tear this dump apart and find what I need anyway. Or you could break your stupid little policy and save us both the trouble. Or I could grab you from your little chair there and bitch-slap you until your head rings like a church bell on Sunday. It's up to you, but I gotta tell you I haven't bitch-slapped anybody in a while and I'm really looking forward to it."

The woman looked at me.

"She's trying to quit smoking," I said. "So she's a mite testy."

"What's it gonna be, babe?" Jane said. "Save us a trip to a judge or I really lose my fucking temper and go Braveheart on you."

"If we get a court order the publicity will be negative and I don't think you want or need that," I said.

The woman sighed. "What do you want to know?"

In an office, the woman fished out a file from a cabinet and quickly scanned it. "Amanda Felton," she said. "Age fourteen. Is she who you're referring to?"

"Yes," I said. "When was she here for the abortion?"

"August 10th."

"Two weeks or so before school started back up," I said. "Was she alone?"

"I don't know," the woman said. "She came in alone, but somebody may have driven her. That happens a lot and the driver waits outside."

"And her father didn't know?" I said.

"That's correct," the woman said.

"Were there any complications?" I said.

The woman scanned the file again. "No, none," she said. "Amanda was perfectly healthy when she got here and when she left."

I nodded. "Okay, we're done. Thank you."

The woman looked at Jane. "We do breast exams here," she said. "When was the last time you had them examined?"

"Lady, if anybody is going to squeeze my boobs it's going to be that hunk from the X-Men movies. The one with the sideburns."

★ ★ ★ ★ ★

Jane and I sat side-by-side in the new chairs in front of my trailer.

"Where's Regan?" Jane said.

"Last-minute practice run with Oz," I said. "Her road test is in a few days."

"Let me think out loud here for a minute," Jane said. "James Crawford is eighteen now, but was seventeen before July. He and Amanda Felton spend time together because she sits his baby sister. He drives her to and from; their hormones go haywire as teenage hormones are apt to do and bing, bam, boom she gets knocked up. Before that happens he buys her a cheap pair of earrings that she stuck in her case because Daddy bought her the real thing and she doesn't want him to find out about her backseat romance. Once she realizes she's pregnant the back and forth calls start and she borrows her uncle's cell to call James over the 4th of July. He or she makes an appointment with Family Planning and the baby is aborted. Somehow Norman Felton found out about it and . . . drives to the high school and beats the Montero kid with a baseball bat. Afterward it's discovered that Amanda Felton is missing and hasn't been heard from since. It doesn't add up or make sense, does it?"

"Suppose somehow Felton thought the Montero kid was the one who got his daughter pregnant," I said. "Then it makes sense."

"How do you confuse a skinny Latin kid with that monster James Crawford?" Jane said. "Even Mr. Magoo could tell them apart."

I pulled out the e-cigarette and puffed on it while I mulled things over.

"And where is the girl?" Jane said.

"Want some coffee?" I said.

"I want a good stiff drink is what I want," Jane said.

"Me, too."

Jane looked at me. "Sorry. Coffee is fine."

I went into my trailer for a moment to carry out the pot and mugs. Back outside, I poured and sat. Jane lit a real smoke and started to sip.

"If the girl isn't dead, why hasn't she come forward?" I said. "She wasn't kidnapped, and except for some blood spatter on the rug and her missing earring there are no visible signs that she was murdered."

"You think she ran away?" Jane said.

"Yes."

"I do, too."

"Because?"

Jane hit on the cigarette and exhaled through her nose. "Shame," she said. "Amanda has been raised by her father and they're all they got. Each other. She's a Daddy's girl and he would die for her. She got pregnant and he found out about it and in her eyes there is no greater sin. She can't live with the shame so she runs away."

"Are you talking about Amanda and her father or Regan and me?" I said.

"Regan is nineteen, Jack," Jane said. "There will be boys."

"Nineteen, but emotionally younger than Mark," I said.

"And the boys know that how?" Jane said. "When one of them takes advantage of her young emotional state and he tries to do the no-no, what are you gonna do, Jack? What are you gonna do?"

I felt as if I'd been punched in the gut. "Are you trying to get me to think like Norman Felton again?" I said.

"Are you?"

"Yes."

"So what are you gonna do, Jack?"

I sipped coffee and took a hit on the e-cigarette.

"I'm going to break the law," I said. "Want to break it with me?"

"Why not?" Jane said. "I'm retiring anyway. When?"

"Sunday after the next game," I said. "No uniform."

"And the next three days?"

"Go over everything again and again and maybe find something we missed."

"And you're doing . . . ?"

"Keeping a promise," I said.

Jane tossed her spent cigarette and looked at me. "Jack, when—and I say when and not if—that boy puts the moves on your little girl, go easy on him. He could be a really nice guy, and we were that age once."

"You're not just another pretty face, are you?" I said.

Jane gave me her best smirk. "Hell, I've been telling you that for years, Bekker."

THIRTY-FOUR

Our plane landed at Kennedy Airport and it was just a short ride to the hospice in Queens where Joey was staying. Originally part of the United Nations housing complex back in the forties and fifties, it was sold and converted into condos and the hospice that is almost as large as a small hospital.

Regan wore jeans with a teal pullover shirt, black sneakers and her diamond earrings. Her hair was pulled back ponytail-fashion and there was just a hint of eyeliner around her eyes.

We had just carry-on bags so we scooted past baggage claim and got in line for a cab. I told the dispatcher it would be a short ride so I would tip extra for the driver's trouble.

While we waited, I looked at Regan.

She looked back. "What?" she said.

"Do me a favor and don't tell me about them," I said.

"Them who?"

"Boys."

"Boys? What boys? Do you know something I don't?"

"Yeah," I said. "I know that the older I get, the more I realize just how little I know."

"Dad, have you lost what's left of your teeny, tiny mind?"

"Our cab's here," I said.

The hospice looked more like a very upscale motel than a place for recovering hospital patients. The horseshoe-shaped building was blue with white trim and a large front lawn with beds of flowers that led the way to a drop-off/pick-up roundabout outside the front entrance.

I tipped the driver an extra twenty and we rolled our carry-on luggage into the comfortably ornate lobby. A woman dressed in white whom we didn't see until she appeared from somewhere greeted us as we entered. "May I help you?" she said with a pleasant smile.

"We're here to see Josephine Fureal," I said.

The woman smiled at me. "You mean Joey?"

"Yes."

"Follow me."

The woman led us through a maze of carpeted hallways to a set of glass doors that opened up to a courtyard garden about a half acre in size. Joey was seated on a bench in front of a lily pond. Buddy sat by her side.

"Visitors, Joey," the woman said.

Joey turned, looked at me and smiled.

"Mr. Bekker . . . I mean Jack," she said as she stood and gave me a warm hug.

Joey was a little thinner than the last time I saw her. She wore no makeup and a Yankees baseball cap covered her blonde hair, but her eyes were still bright and clear and her voice was solid.

"This is my daughter, Regan," I said.

Joey gave Regan a quick once-over. "Oh my, aren't you pretty," she said. "I'm amazed your dad doesn't have a head of gray hair from beating the boys away."

"Thanks," Regan said. "And so are you."

"Not so much these days, but thanks anyway," Joey said. "Say hi to Buddy."

Buddy gave me a hand lick and then jumped up on his hind legs to lick Regan on the face.

"So, had dinner yet?" I said.

"Another half hour," Joey said.

"Can we take you out?" I said.

"If the nurse says so."

"She'll say so," I said. "Get changed and I'll be back in half an hour."

"Where are you going?" Regan said.

"Rent a car," I said.

"Come on to my room," Joey said to Regan. "You can help me change."

I walked three blocks from the hospice to Queens Boulevard and then another two blocks to the car rental place I'd spotted on the cab ride from the airport. I rented a full size, four-door sedan. Then I killed time with a spin on Queens Boulevard, grabbed a coffee at a Dairy Queen and drank it in the parking lot. I took a few hits on the e-cigarette while I sipped from the container.

I was thirty minutes late returning to the hospice.

Joey and Regan were in the courtyard with Buddy. Joey had changed into jeans, a green top and a string of pearls, and wore her hair down. They were chatting up a storm and laughing when I arrived.

What I wanted to happen, happened. Two young women with a history of tragic events came together out of the shared knowledge of pain and fear, and bonded.

"You said thirty minutes," Regan said.

"I got lost," I said.

Joey gave me a knowing look. "I doubt that."

"Shall we go?" I said.

"Where?" Regan said.

"Where grownup girls go to dine," I said.

★ ★ ★ ★ ★

Joey and Regan sat in back while I played chauffer and drove us into Manhattan to the world famous hotel on 59th and Fifth Avenue. The casual dining room still cost an arm and a leg, and parking is twenty bucks an hour. The drive took an hour or so, and the entire time the girls chatted up a storm without so much as a mention or glance my way.

When we finally arrived at the hotel roundabout I got out and held the door open for the girls and they giggled at me.

"No giggling," I said. "This place is for grownups."

Four hours later I returned Joey to the hospice. She was worn out but happy. At the front lobby she gave me a hug and kiss, and the same for Regan.

"Come say good-bye tomorrow?" Joey said. "I'm not due at the hospital until noon."

"You bet," I said.

I reserved two rooms at the Queens Motel a few blocks from the hospice and after we checked in, Regan knocked on my door.

Her eyes were misty. "Every once in a while you're not a total blockhead and get it right, Dad," she said.

"Even a busted clock is right twice a day," I said.

In the morning we said our good-byes in the courtyard. Joey and Regan exchanged cell numbers and whatever, and Joey suggested a photo.

"I didn't bring a camera," I said.

"God, Dad, this isn't 1950," Regan said. "Use my cell phone."

I took a picture of Regan and Joey and then another with Joey's phone. A nurse took one of all three of us plus Buddy, using both phones.

"Time to go, Joey," the nurse said.

Joey pulled me aside and hugged me again. "Thank you," she said.

"For what?"

"For allowing me to forget even if for just a little while that soon I might die."

THIRTY-FIVE

I met Jane in the municipal parking lot adjacent to the beach. She was dressed in black jeans, a black tee shirt and hiking boots. Her heavy gun belt hung low on her hips. I wore similar clothing plus my new hiking boots.

I looked at Jane as she walked toward me. Marilyn Monroe packing heat flashed through my mind.

"We have time for lunch," I said. "That game won't be over until at least three."

We crossed the street and entered the coffee shop. So as not to scare customers under tables at the sight of her Glock, Jane pinned her badge to her tee shirt. We ordered strawberry pancakes, coffee and orange juice.

"You did your nails," I said when I noticed the high shine on Jane's nails.

"Yesterday at the place near my office," Jane said.

"And your hair isn't as frizzed."

"I had it layered out," Jane said. "Same place."

I nodded.

"You really need a haircut," Jane said.

I nodded again.

We ate our pancakes and still had time to kill. I ordered takeout coffee and we crossed the street to the parking lot, went past it to the edge of the beach and found a vacant bench.

Jane lit a cigarette. "I really need to quit," she said.

I put the e-cigarette between my lips. "Me, too."

"So what's your game plan for this?"

"Kick some ass."

"Kicking ass is a game plan?"

"It is when all else fails," I said.

"And what do I do?" Jane said.

"Follow my lead," I said. "And maybe we might walk away knowing more than we do now."

I parked the Marquis in the driveway of a house for sale about a tenth of a mile from the Crawford home. We walked to the house and sat on the front steps.

I glanced at my watch. "Shouldn't be much longer."

Jane lit a cigarette.

"Are you serious about not running for reelection?" I said.

"I think so, yeah. I've had enough, Bekker. Enough of stupid criminals and violent assholes. Enough having to babysit the jail and pretend I care about the lowlife scum occupying it. In general, just plain enough."

"I suppose if I had stayed on the job as long as you I'd probably feel the same," I said. "I know Walt probably does."

"I hear a car," Jane said.

I stood up. Jane stood up beside me. We walked off the front steps and stood in front of Crawford's garage.

A few moments later Crawford's car appeared and turned onto his driveway. Crawford was behind the wheel. James sat beside him. The car screeched to a stop a few feet in front of us.

Red in the face, Crawford emerged from the car and slammed the door behind him. "That's it, Bekker," he said. "I'm calling my lawyer."

James got out the passenger side and looked at me. "Dad, take it easy," he said.

"This is harassment and I won't stand for it," Crawford said. He started walking toward the front door.

I moved to cut him off, and when he turned to me I kicked him in the balls. "No, *this* is harassment," I said.

Crawford went down like a sack of rocks with his hands between his legs.

"Jane, would you incapacitate Mr. Crawford," I said.

Jane looked at Crawford. "I'd say you already did that."

"Sit on him," I said.

Jane cuffed Crawford's hands behind him and then took a seat on the small of his back. "Behave yourself now," she said.

I turned to James. He looked at me with young teenage eyes, scared, confused, almost helpless.

"Okay, football star," I said. "There aren't a dozen guys protecting your ass now. It's just you and me. Show me what you got."

"I . . . I don't think I want to talk to you," James said.

"I wasn't asking," I said as I walked up to him. "Suppose I don't care what you think? What then?"

Face-to-face we were equal height.

"What . . . what do you mean?" James said.

"Quarterback doesn't mean shit in the street," I said. "I'll bet you've never been in one fight in your entire young life."

"I don't see what that has to do with anything," James said.

I punched him in the nose. He staggered backward and hit the hood of the car.

"You're about to find out," I said.

"James!" Crawford yelled.

Jane bounced a few times on Crawford's back. "Hush now," she said.

James spit blood and looked at me. "What do you want?"

"To find out if you're a man or a boy," I said.

"Please, Bekker," Crawford said.

James had no idea what to do.

I showed him with two stiff jabs to the face and a solid right hook to the gut. He folded, and I spun him around and slammed his face into the hood of the car.

"That looked like it hurt," Jane said.

"Bekker, I'm begging you," Crawford said. "Please."

"I told you to hush," Jane said and bounced a few more times on Crawford's back.

I grabbed James by his right arm, twisted and raised it above his head. "Is this your million-dollar ticket to college?" I said. "One more twist and you'll never throw another football again."

"Stop it, Bekker! Please just stop it!" Crawford shouted.

"Gimme a reason," I said.

"All right, okay," Crawford sobbed. "I'll give you a reason. Just let him alone. He's just a kid, for God's sake."

"So are Montero and Amanda Felton," I said. "Jane, let him up."

James sat on the sofa with an ice pack on his face and another on his right shoulder. Crawford sat next to him. Jane and I stood.

"Where is your daughter?" I said.

"Mainland with my sister," Crawford said.

"Okay, let's start with you, Mr. Crawford," I said. "That was you who broke into the Felton home and later hit the sheriff with a log in the woods."

Crawford nodded. "Yes."

James looked at his father. "Dad? What?"

"Well, what was I supposed to do, let you piss away college and a chance at the pros over some cheap pair of earrings?" Crawford said. "They would have found them. They would have traced them back to you, and I . . ."

"So what?" James said. "I bought them, but I didn't give them to her. Steff wanted to give them to her for her birthday."

"Your sister gave them to Amanda?" I said.

"Yeah, when she turned fourteen," James said. "What, you thought I gave them to her?"

"Mr. Crawford, obviously we surprised you that day, but why were you going to vacuum the rug?" I said.

"What are you talking about, vacuum?" Crawford said. "I was going to check her jewelry box in her room."

"Mr. Crawford, your boot size is a thirteen, a full size larger than your shoe size," I said. "I was stumped for a bit until I bought a pair of my own and the clerk told me to buy a size larger because you need the room for thick hiking socks to prevent blisters."

Crawford nodded. "I'm not denying I entered the house for those earrings, but that's all I did, and I did it to protect my idiot son."

"From what?" James said.

"From what?" Crawford said. Then he turned and slapped James across his already swollen face. "From the newspapers getting ahold of the story that you got a fourteen-year-old girl pregnant and took her for an abortion, that's from what. The sheriff could arrest you right now for that and then what happens to you?"

"Is that what you think?" James said.

"I checked your cell phone," Crawford said. "I got suspicious when Amanda called you on it and not the hard line. I saw the number for Family Planning. You borrowed the car and drove her there a few weeks before school started. I used a company van and followed you. Deny it and you're a liar on top of everything else."

"I don't deny it," James said. "I did drive her there. She was scared and asked me for help. I drove her there, but I never touched her."

"Are you saying you weren't the father?" I said.

James looked at me. "Jesus Christ, she's fourteen years old," he said.

"Do you know who is?" I said.

"She wouldn't tell me," James said. "She was really scared her father would find out. She wouldn't tell me who . . . the father is. Was."

"The Montero kid?" I said.

James looked at me and lowered his eyes.

"Time to man up, James," I said. "Tell me what you know."

"Wait," Crawford said. "Do we need a lawyer? My son's college career is at stake here, maybe a shot at the pros."

"I don't need a lawyer, Dad," James said. "I'm guilty of nothing except being a coward."

"What are you talking about?" Crawford said. "Anybody who plays . . ."

"Mr. Crawford, let him speak," Jane said. She looked at James. "Go ahead, son."

"I like to check the conditions of the field before a game," James said. "I know it was just a preseason game, but I like to check anyway. I don't want to catch my spikes on a rough spot and blow out a knee."

James paused to adjust the ice on his shoulder. "Need more?" I said.

"Not yet."

"Go ahead then," Jane said.

"I borrowed Dad's car and drove Steff to my aunt's house to stay overnight," James said. "Then I swung by the field. The Montero kid was by himself hitting fungos. Know what that is?"

"I do," I said.

"Oh, yeah, that's right," James said. "I guess you do. So anyway, I asked him if I could hit a few and he went to the outfield, and then we switched off and he hit some to me. I told you about my vision thing, right?"

239

"Yes."

"He smacked one good and I misjudged it and it went through a window," James said. "I went to check the window and the next thing I know Mr. Felton is there and screaming his head off. I knew somehow he found out about the . . . about what happened and I panicked. All I could think about was . . . myself. My scholarship. My chance to play big-time football. I ran away. I ran away and left that kid to get his brains beat out and he didn't do a damn thing except be there when Mr. Felton showed up."

"Why didn't you tell me all this?" Crawford said.

"I told you, I was afraid," James said. "Mr. Bekker, can I get some more ice now?"

I nodded.

James stood and went to the kitchen.

Crawford looked at me. "Are we under arrest?" he said.

"Not at the moment," I said. "Where did you get the key to the Felton home?"

"I don't have a key," Crawford said. "I went to the back door. I was going to break a window. The door was open. I went in."

"Did you try the front door?" I said.

"No."

James returned with fresh ice and took his seat.

"Any idea how Mr. Felton found out about Amanda?" I said.

James shook his head.

"When did you last see her?" I said.

"A few days before the . . . a few days before," James said. "I was doing my roadwork and she was in front of her house. I asked her how she was and she said everything was okay. Then I went back to my roadwork."

"Do you know her friends? Maybe one of them is hiding her?" I said.

"No, but maybe Steff would know a few," James suggested.

"Mr. Crawford, when are you picking her up?" I said.

"Now, if I'm allowed."

"Mr. Crawford, that little B&E you pulled and withholding evidence will be forgotten and dismissed if you bring your daughter to the sheriff's department for questioning," I said.

"My son?" Crawford said.

I nodded. "It's cool."

Crawford stood up. "I'll meet you there as soon as I pick her up. James, you stay home and keep icing that shoulder."

I looked at James. "Sorry about the rough stuff."

"I had it coming," James said.

"For what it's worth, I needed to scare you into coming clean," I said. "I wouldn't have really hurt you. I'm sorry if I did."

"If that was a bluff I'd like to see you when you're really mad," James said.

"No, no you wouldn't," Jane said and winked at James. "Good luck with college."

James nodded. "Thanks."

We turned to follow Crawford out of the house.

"Mr. Bekker?" James said.

I turned around.

"Come see me play sometime?"

"Sure."

THIRTY-SIX

Stephanie Crawford was a tiny little girl of nine years old. She had dark hair and eyes and weighed all of eighty pounds.

She was scared to death when her father led her by the hand into the sheriff's department.

"It's all right, honey," Jane said when Crawford brought Stephanie into the office. "You've done nothing wrong. We just want to ask for your help. Okay?"

"My help?" Stephanie said in a soft, birdlike voice.

Jane sat on the edge of her desk. "Please sit down. Mr. Crawford, you sit next to her."

Crawford and Stephanie took seats.

I stood behind Jane's desk. Stephanie looked at me. "Who is he?" she said.

"My friend John Bekker," Jane said. "He helps me sometimes."

"He needs a haircut," Stephanie said.

Jane looked at me. "Yes, he does. Why don't you tell him so?"

"You need a haircut," Stephanie told me. "Short like my daddy."

I nodded.

"Now Stephanie, do you know why you're here?" Jane said.

"My daddy says you want to ask me questions about Amanda," Stephanie said.

"That's correct, sweetheart," Jane said. "About Amanda. She babysits you a lot, doesn't she?"

Stephanie nodded.

"So you two must talk a lot?" Jane said. "About this and that, right?"

Stephanie nodded again.

"Put on your thinking cap for me, okay?" Jane said. "Did Amanda ever tell you about her friends and maybe a boy that she liked or who liked her?"

"A boy?" Stephanie said. "Like a boyfriend?"

"Uh huh, like a boyfriend," Jane said.

Stephanie shook her head. "I don't think so, no. Mostly we talked about our favorite TV shows and movies and sometimes dolls. I have a lot of dolls and so did she when she was little."

"What about her friends? Did she ever talk about them or bring any with her?" Jane said.

"Not that I remember," Stephanie said. "She's a cheerleader at school. Sometimes she would show me how to do cheers. We'd practice."

Jane nodded. "You liked her a lot. That's why you bought her earrings."

Stephanie nodded.

"I'm going to ask your daddy to take you home now, but I want you to do something for me, okay?" Jane said.

Another head nod.

"I want you to think real hard and try to remember if Amanda ever talked about a friend or boy and try to remember names," Jane said. "Can you do that for me?"

"Yes," Stephanie said.

Crawford stood and took Stephanie's hand. "Let's go home, honey," he said.

Stephanie looked at me. "Don't forget about the haircut," she said.

After Crawford and Stephanie left the office, Jane flopped behind her desk. "Christ, I could use a drink," she said.

I looked at my watch. "Let me give Walt a call and I'll buy."

The Red Barn wasn't exactly a cop bar, but it was as close to one as there was inside the county. Dark with a long mahogany bar, the Barn had tables and booths and a small dance floor for those compelled to use the jukebox.

We took a booth by a tinted window. The bartender came around from behind the bar and walked over to us. "Lieutenant, is that you? It's been a while."

"I guess so; it's captain now," Walt said.

"Oh, yeah, I read about that in the papers about a year ago," the bartender said.

"Do you know County Sheriff Jane Morgan?" Walt said.

"Haven't had the pleasure," the bartender said. He looked at me. "You I remember. You used to be a regular and then you disappeared."

"I got sober," I said.

"Too bad. You were a good tipper."

"Scotch and soda for me," Walt said.

"Jack and diet Coke," Jane said.

"Ginger ale and ice," I said.

The bartender nodded and returned to the bar.

"So, what is this little parley about?" Walt said.

We waited for the drinks to arrive and then Jane brought Walt up to speed.

"Son of a bitch, I didn't think it possible at this point, but the girl just might be alive," Walt said.

"It's more of a possibility tonight than yesterday," Jane said. "Even if it's a long shot at best."

"No money, credit cards or phone—where could she go?" Walt said.

Jane and Walt looked at each other. "Homeless shelters and churches," they said in unison.

"Three shelters in the city and about a dozen or so churches," Walt said.

"Four shelters in the county, at least thirty or more churches," Jane said.

Walt pulled out his cell phone and punched in a number. "It's me," he said. "Get every detective and have them meet me in my office in one hour. No arguments, no excuses." He hit end and dumped the phone into a pocket.

"I see you're an understanding boss," I said.

"That reminds me," Walt said. "I spoke to some members of the review board. At worst they won't approve reinstatement. At best they will but with reduction from sergeant to detective. Inside a year you'll be back to sergeant, two to lieutenant."

Jane looked at me. "Don't look so happy about it," she said.

"You did everything you could, Jack," Walt said. "My guys and Jane's will hit every church and shelter in the county looking for the girl. Want to tag along?"

"I'm going to go home and do nothing," I said.

"That will be the day," Jane said.

THIRTY-SEVEN

I was staring into space when Regan came up behind me, then walked around and sat on my lap. "Want to see some pictures, Dad?"

"Sure."

"Want some coffee to go with them?"

"Why not?"

"Be right back."

Regan stood up and went inside for a few minutes. She returned with a mug of coffee and her laptop.

I wanted a real cigarette, but I settled for the e-smoke and puffed away as Regan opened her photos file. There were some pictures of her and Buddy, Joey and Buddy, and her, Joey and Buddy in the courtyard gardens.

"When did this happen?" I said.

"When you were stalling and left us alone," Regan said. "Here are the ones you took."

Regan and Joey smiled brightly in the photograph. Buddy was by Joey's side.

"Did you send this to her?" I said.

"Not yet," Regan said. "I wanted to do a little touching up first. I'll send them now."

"I almost forgot to ask," I said. "When is your road test?"

"Three days," Regan said. "I asked Oz to reschedule so I'd have time to practice with the compact."

"Good idea," I said. "Let's go get one."

"Now?" Regan said. "It will be dark soon. I doubt they'll be open."

"First thing in the morning, then," I said.

"Okay. Here comes Oz now. I'll tell him about the compact."

Oz tossed a log into the bonfire and took his seat beside me. The sun was going down and a cool breeze blew in off the ocean.

"I don't get you," he said. "If they find that girl it's because of you, and you're moping around here like a beaten wet dog."

"I'm fine," I said.

"Bullshit," Oz said. "I know fine when I see it and this isn't it. Is it Janet? When she coming home?"

"I don't know," I said. "I've lost track of time. A few days, I think."

"And what are you going to do about it?"

"I don't know that either."

"What do you know?" Oz said.

"Not a lot."

"At least you smart enough to admit you're stupid," Oz said. "That's more than most."

"It doesn't quite add up," I said. "There is something I'm missing. A link or piece of the puzzle that would make it all make sense."

"Can you solve it from your chair?" Oz said.

"No."

"Then shut up and enjoy that beautiful sunset right in front of us," Oz said.

"How did she get off the island?" I said. "She could have walked to the ferry and rode it to the mainland and then what? Where did she go from there?"

Oz stood, tossed another log onto the fire and took his seat.

"What did she use for money?" I said. "Her cash is in her

247

piggybank."

"Maybe one of her friends took her in?" Oz suggested.

"And is hiding her for almost a month?" I said. "Even after the news reports of her father's death?"

"Maybe she too afraid to come forward?" Oz said.

"Or maybe she can't?" I said.

"I wasn't going to go there," Oz said. "I'd like to think at this point the girl is still alive."

"Yeah," I said.

"So you going to just sit there all night like some statue?"

"I'm waiting."

"Want me to wait with you?"

"For a while," I said.

Regan stuck her head out the door of the trailer. "I'm making spaghetti and meatballs," she said. "Oz, are you staying?"

"Garlic rolls?" Oz said.

"Of course."

"Set me a plate, girl," Oz said. "Oz is coming to dinner."

Four hours later I sat alone at the new table with a mug of coffee and the e-cigarette for company.

Jane called first. "Struck out, Bekker," she said. "No one's seen her anywhere. We even checked the bus and train stations and the airport."

"Now what?" I said.

"Walt and my department are teaming up for some public service announcements on TV and radio," Jane said. "We got them to do the spots for free as a public service."

"Okay," I said. "Any news on the Montero kid?"

"I almost forgot: there is," Jane said. "He's out of danger after emergency surgery and the doctors think he'll pull through."

"Good. You tell his father?"

"The man hasn't left his hospital room."

"Okay," I said.

"Are you all right?"

"Just tired."

"Go get some sleep."

"I will," I said. "Do me a favor—call Walt and tell him no need to call me."

"Sure."

"Goodnight then," I said.

"Hey, Bekker, you did good."

I hung up my phone and sat there for a few more minutes.

I did good.

That's something you say to someone who finished in second place.

THIRTY-EIGHT

I took Regan and Oz to breakfast in town. We walked. Afterward we walked to the car rental place on Main Street and rented a compact for Regan's road test. She drove me back to the beach before going off with Oz to practice.

"Let me check my laptop real quick before we go, Oz," Regan said. "I'm expecting an email."

I took my chair while Regan went inside. Oz stood beside the compact.

Regan emerged with the laptop. "Dad, look," she said. "From Joey."

Regan set the laptop on the table. Joey had photo-shopped the picture I took of her, Regan and Buddy by darkening the background, spotlighting them and adding a neon frame.

I stared at the photo. Regan's earrings glistened. So did Joey's.

"Dad?" Regan said.

"Son of a bitch," I said.

"What? Dad? Is something wrong?" Regan said.

"Can you print that?" I said.

"I was lucky Aunt Janet gave me the laptop when she got a new one," Regan said.

"You can use mine," Oz said.

"You have a printer?" I said to Oz.

Oz shook his head at me. "Come on, Regan," he said. "Let's print a copy for Mr. Stone Age and be on our way."

While Oz and Regan walked down to his trailer, I grabbed

my cell phone and called Jane.

"Do you still have all that stuff from the Felton home?" I said. "From his desk—all those records?"

"I do," Jane said.

"Are you in your office?"

"I am."

"Stay there."

I picked up two containers of coffee on the way into Jane's office and set them on her desk when I entered. "That file Felton kept with all his transactions, you got it?" I said.

"I do, but . . . ?"

"Let's take another look."

"The box is at the conference table."

Norman Felton was a meticulous man. He kept impeccable records of his finances. He accounted for every penny of his income and expenditures going back five years.

I went through every scrap of paper he hand-wrote and receipt he itemized, and we made separate piles by category.

"Take a look at this," I said. I removed the folded printed photo of Joey and Regan and set it on the desk.

"Who is the girl?" Jane said.

"A sick friend from Hawaii," I said. "We went to visit her last week."

"Pretty girl."

"See Regan's earrings?" I said.

"I do. What about . . . ?"

"I paid twelve hundred dollars for those earrings and I have the receipt in my wallet to prove it," I said. "Norman Felton kept records of his finances like a CPA; where is the receipt for Amanda's earrings? The earrings in the photo of her and her father. This photo." I pulled the photo of Amanda and Norman

Felton with her brand new diamond earrings and set it on the table.

Jane looked at it and then looked at me.

"Look at both photos and tell me what you see," I said. "Or don't see."

Jane set the two photos side by side and looked at them. Then she turned her head and I could see the lights come on in her eyes.

"That's right," I said. "I'm not in the photo of Regan and Joey because I took it. So who took the photo of Amanda and her father?"

"Someone else," Jane said. "Someone close."

I pulled out a stack of phone bills from the file. "Check out this number," I said.

Jane's eyes traced my finger.

"Son of a fucking bitch," she said.

"Exactly right," I said. "Son of a fucking bitch."

THIRTY-NINE

Lieutenant Ralph Franks of the Rhode Island State Police took charge of the raid on Robert Felton's home. A judge issued a search warrant and Franks held it in his hand as he rang the doorbell and then pounded his fist on the door.

It was after midnight. The house, set back on a country road, was dark and quiet.

Franks rang the bell a second time. A light on the second floor came on.

"He's up," Franks said into his shirt-mounted radio. "Hold positions until my order."

A dozen armed state police officers held positions at the front and rear doors of the large home.

Jane and I stood beside Franks.

"I'll allow you in as observers," Franks said to us. "But you're background noise and take no aggression. Agreed?"

"Yes," I said.

Jane nodded.

We heard Robert Felton come to the door. He took a moment, likely to look through the peephole, and then the door opened. He stood there wearing a blue robe over pajamas. "Yes?" Felton said. "What is it?"

"Mr. Felton, I'm Lieutenant Franks, State Police," Franks said. "I have a warrant to search your home."

"Whatever for?"

"Please step aside and allow my men to enter," Franks said.

Felton looked past Franks at me. "Bekker?" he said.

"Mr. Felton, step aside," Franks said.

Felton moved away from the door. Franks walked past him, turned and nodded to his men out front. "Entering the house," he said into his radio to the men in the rear.

"Mind telling me what this is about?" Felton said.

Franks gave him the warrant. "Read it for yourself."

"Is there any reason I can't read this in my den?" Felton said.

"As long as I go with you," Franks said. "Where is your computer?"

"My bedroom on a desk."

Franks nodded to his men and they took off for the second floor.

"The den is this way," Felton said.

We followed him down a hallway to the den. It was a large room with an oak desk, bookcases filled with books, a globe, a small television and a well-stocked liquor cabinet.

"Anybody want a drink?" Felton said.

"No," Franks said.

"May I?" Felton said.

Franks nodded.

Felton opened the liquor cabinet and filled a glass with a few ounces of bourbon. "Okay to sit?" he said.

"Go ahead," Franks said.

Felton took a seat behind the desk. He glanced at the warrant. "This doesn't say specifically what you're looking for."

"I think you know," Franks said.

Felton took a sip of bourbon and looked at me. "I think I always knew you would figure it out," he said. "I tried to throw you off the track by implicating that kid and it might have worked on someone else, but not you. You're one of those guys always prowling around who never quits, willing to sacrifice all to get to the bottom of it. Did you get to the bottom of it?"

I nodded.

Felton raised his glass to me and took another sip.

"I'm a very sick man, Bekker," Felton said. "I don't want to be, but I am. My wife knew it. That's why she left me before I started molesting my daughters."

I nodded again. "When did you start molesting Amanda?"

"Does it matter?"

"Why didn't she tell her father?" I said.

"You convince a young child that their parents will blame them and hate them forever if they find out and a kid keeps it quiet," Felton said.

There was a knock on the door. Franks opened it and one of his men poked his head in. "Computer is loaded with kiddy porn, LT. Some of it is the girl," he said.

"Thank you," Franks said. "Pack it up for the lab."

The officer nodded and closed the door.

"Like I said, I'm a very sick man," Felton said.

"Did you know she was pregnant?" I said. "And had an abortion."

"No."

"Do you still have the key to your brother's house?" I said.

"Key?" Felton said. "I've never had a key."

Jane looked at me.

Felton took another sip of bourbon. "I still can't figure out how my brother found out," he said. "Amanda wouldn't have told him after having the abortion. She was too afraid of what he might think of her."

"Your brother was an old-fashioned kind of guy," I said. "He kept records and receipts of everything. There was no record or receipt for the diamond earrings because you bought them. He kept phone bills in a file for a year at a time. I looked at the last three months' worth of phone bills. The old-fashioned kind of bill where they list numbers considered long-distance calls.

Amanda called Family Planning in late June. He saw the number on the bill in August and didn't recognize it, and called it himself. Norman also saw the extra calls to James Crawford's cell number, and called it and wanted to talk to James, but James was at the high-school field and wouldn't be home for hours. Your brother stewed for a while and then decided to go to the school and confront James. He was out of control by the time he arrived and it's not too difficult to imagine the rest."

Felton nodded. "They won't give me the death penalty, will they?"

"My guess is life without parole," I said. "Isolation the first ten years to keep you from getting shanked by the lifers who hate a short-eyes."

Felton downed the rest of the bourbon and stood up. "Too bad," he said.

"Mr. Felton, sit down," Franks said.

Felton stuck his hand in his right pocket and pulled out a small caliber revolver.

Franks drew his weapon. "Put that down," he said.

Felton stuck the revolver in his mouth.

"I really did love Amanda," he said.

"Felton, no!" Franks yelled as Felton pulled the trigger.

"When did you figure out that phone bill thing?" Jane said.

We were in an all-night coffee shop near the state police barracks.

"This morning," I said. "After I connected the dots with Regan's photo and the lack of a receipt for the earrings."

"He took the coward's way out," Jane said.

"He was a sick individual," I said.

Jane sipped coffee. "He said he never had a key."

"I believe him."

"Franks said I can have copies of all information found on

Felton's computer," Jane said. "I'm not sure I want it."

"I don't blame you," I said. "Let's grab a coffee to go. We have a long drive."

"You want to drive some of the way?" Jane said.

"It's been a long time since I drove a cruiser," I said.

"Think of it as an old shoe," Jane said.

Yeah. On an old foot.

FORTY

Jane drove for two hours before I took over and drove the rest of the way. Around four in the morning she nodded off against the window. I let her sleep, stopped once on the highway for coffee and reached the ferry by sunup.

Before entering the entrance ramp for the boat, I ducked into the coffee shop at the end of the pier and picked up two containers with two lemon Danish. When I returned to the cruiser Jane was awake and smoking a cigarette.

"You drove all night?" she said when I got behind the wheel.

"I did," I said and handed her a bag.

Jane grabbed a coffee, opened the lid and took a sip. "Why are we here?"

"I forgot an important piece of evidence," I said.

Jane dug out her lemon Danish and took a bite. "I feel like I could sleep for a week," she said. "And I just might."

I drove the cruiser onto the ferry. We took our coffee outside, stood on deck and felt the morning sun and salt-sea air on our faces.

"So what evidence did you forget?" Jane said.

"The last piece of the puzzle."

"Are you going to tell me, or is it show and tell?"

"More like wait and see."

I parked the cruiser in the Felton driveway. The other cruiser and yellow tape had been removed. I looked at Jane.

"Go around back," I said. "I'll meet you there."

"I don't . . ." Jane said.

"Humor me in my old age," I said.

Jane got out and walked around to the back of the house. I went to the front door, put my finger on the doorbell and held it for a count of ten.

I heard a noise from inside the house and ran around back where Amanda surprised Jane as she came over the fence like a gazelle and made a mad dash for the woods.

"Amanda, wait!" Jane shouted as she took off after the girl.

Amanda made it across the street to the fringe of the woods before Jane tackled her at the knees and they went down hard. Amanda kicked and screamed and put up a hell of a fight, but Jane pinned her down and held the girl tight.

"It's all right, honey," Jane said. "You're safe now. No one can hurt you anymore."

"My uncle," Amanda sobbed. "He . . . he . . ."

"He's gone, honey and he's never coming back," Jane said. "Ever."

"My father's dead," Amanda sobbed.

"I know," Jane said.

"My uncle did . . . he made me . . ." Amanda said between sobs.

"Listen to me," Jane said. "Your uncle is gone and he can never hurt you or anyone else ever again. I promise you that."

Amanda grabbed Jane around the neck. Jane lifted the girl into her arms and carried her across the street. "She's been on this side of Midnight all along," she said.

And I watched as the toughest woman I've ever met in my life hugged Amanda and cried like a baby.

FORTY-ONE

I tossed several logs onto the bonfire and returned to my new chair. It was breaking in nicely, but still had a way to go to replace the comfort of the old one.

Oz said, "If that fire gets any bigger they could see it from outer space."

"When did you figure out she was in the house?" Walt said.

"No key, vacuum moved, money intact," I said. "It was obvious there at the end that she was hiding in plain sight. She didn't know what else to do or where to go so she did nothing and went nowhere. She was smart enough to keep the drapes closed and not turn on lights after dark. If someone came near the house she'd go out the back, hop the fence and hide in the woods until they left. Us included."

"Not so obvious, Bekker," Jane said. "Give yourself some credit. A dozen trained eyes looked at the evidence and no one else figured out the phone numbers or that Robert Felton bought the earrings."

"When I talk to the board on your behalf a story like this goes a long way," Walt said. "Maybe you'll even keep the sergeant stripes."

I looked at Jane. "Every once in a while the job is worth doing," I said. "Still not going to run for reelection?"

Jane leaned in close to me. "What happened this morning out there, I mean that doesn't have to go past us, right?" she said.

"Oh, hell, Jane," Walt said. "I would have cried, too."

Jane sat back in her chair and glared at Walt. "I had something in my eyes," she said.

"They're called tears," Walt said.

"You know, you don't run for sheriff again you could always partner up with Mr. Stone Age here," Oz said. "He need somebody to keep him in line and I'm getting too old for the job, and he a pain in the ass anyway."

Jane looked at me.

"Where's Regan?" Oz said.

"Coming," Regan said as she stepped out of the trailer with the chocolate cake she'd baked.

"What's this for?" I said.

"Celebrate," Regan said. "I got my license today, remember?"

"I do and I'll take a big piece," I said.

Robert Felton's ex-wife said she would take Amanda in and raise her as one of her own. It would have to clear Social Services and a judge would have to sign off on it, but I didn't see that as a problem. Amanda would need years of therapy, but her living nightmare was over and with time, love and understanding she just might be able to put it all in the past.

Yeah, every once in a while the job is worth doing.

Regan started slicing up the cake.

"Make it a really big piece," I said.

FORTY-TWO

I glanced at my watch. It was just past ten in the morning. I took a seat at the patio table and sipped coffee while I waited for Regan. The e-cigarette was in my pocket and I left it there.

I was being weaned.

Regan was taking longer than usual, but the bathroom was small and women need a lot of space for all their stuff. Looking for a house for us wasn't out of the question if and when I did or didn't work things out with Janet.

I was waiting for her call.

My cell phone rang at fifteen minutes past ten. I let it ring three times before I answered it.

"Jack?" Janet said.

"How did the training go?" I said.

"Fine," Janet said. "I think we need to talk."

"I agree," I said. "Let me start."

"No, I should . . ."

"I love you and owe you more than I can ever repay," I said. "And you were right about want and not need. No relationship should be based on need."

"Jack, I know what I . . ."

"I know about Clayton visiting you in Chicago," I said. "And I don't care about that. You probably slept together and I don't really care about that either. I realized something this past month and it's this; I can't give you what you want. I'm not nine to five, dinner at six, and the news at seven material. I am what I am and I do what I do, and because I do what I do sometimes a young girl gets a shot at having a life. What you do is important, real important, but so is what I do, just on a different level. I have to go now. Regan and I are catching a plane to New York. Think it over and we'll talk in a few days when I get back. Okay?"

Janet was silent for a few seconds.

"Okay, Jack," she finally said. "In a few days."

I hung up and stuck the phone in my pocket. I thought about the e-cigarette, but let it stay where it was on the table.

The weaning was on the winning side of the addiction.

A few minutes later, Regan came out with a very unhappy Molly locked inside a pink carrying case. "Are you sure the airlines will let me keep her under the seat?" Regan said.

I stood up. "I'm sure."

"And the motel allows cats?"

"I'm sure about that, too," I said. "They even supply a litter box and food bowls."

Molly voiced her opinion on being locked inside the carrying case and let go with a loud angry meow.

"Then let's go see Joey and celebrate her birthday," Regan said.

I grabbed our luggage and headed toward the Marquis.

"Dad?"

"What?"

"Let's take my car," my grown-up daughter said. "I'll drive."

I nodded. "Okay."

"And there's still time for you to get a haircut," Regan said as she opened the rear door of her car and placed Molly on the back seat.

ABOUT THE AUTHOR

Al Lamanda is the author of the mystery novels *Dunston Falls, Walking Homeless, Running Homeless, Sunset, Sunrise* and *First Light. Sunset* was nominated for the Edgar Award for Best Mystery of 2012. *Sunrise* was voted Best Crime Novel of 2013 by the Maine Writers and Publishers Alliance. An avid weight-lifter and boxer, Al spends much of his free time looking after his very lazy Maine Coon cat.